MURDER IN THE SHALLOWS

A Violet Carlyle Mystery

BETH BYERS

For Jeremiah & Emily
Bwahahahahaha

SUMMARY

July 1924.

Violet and Jack go for a simple day on the water. They little expect their day of sun and fun to end with finding a body in the water.

The mystery of what happened to the young man in the shallows posses them both, and they unite in their desire to find out more. Will they be able to discover why Jack's one-time friend was killed? Who would have done this and why?

CHAPTER ONE

*J*ack led the way through the crowded train station as they hurried to reach the train. They were late—all Vi's fault, of course. He was too respectable and prepared to be late for the train if she weren't involved.

Violet winced as she thought back to her morning. She should have been wiser. She never thought, of course, that she'd spend so much time talking to her wayward ward, Ginny, about her failing classes. Violet had imagined she'd only tell the girl that a tutor was coming, to be good, give Vi's spaniel extra loves while she was gone, and torture her twin, Victor. Instead, Vi had been forced to listen to the well-justified woes of Ginny, who had been dubbed Lady Guttersnipe by her spoiled classmates and even some of the teachers. The staff would be hearing from the 'Lady' version of Violet Carlyle.

How to handle the rest of Ginny's woes? Violet had no idea. Nothing had made her feel more helpless than being caught floundering as Ginny poured her troubles out. Somehow, Violet had stumbled through the conversation and had ended it in a flurry of dressing and a need for a stiff drink.

It certainly didn't help that Jack had been early to meet Violet, so he had to wait even longer for her as she dressed. Victor had 'helped' by harassing her from the moment she had put on her dress to the moment she ran out of her room with her hat and hatpin in hand.

"I'm sorry, I'm sorry," she called as she ran down the stairs.

"We might miss the train," Jack said in a tight voice, "but it'll be fine. There are other trains."

"Will you forgive me?"

His frown disappeared as she stared up at him, and he took her hand, stepping close into her body, and promised, "Always."

There had been a change in his gaze in the last few weeks that had Violet concerned, the same one there as he promised to forgive her. It had sent her mind floundering. She wasn't quite sure what to think of the way he had been acting. The paranoid part of her wondered if something about her was bothering him. Or, maybe he needed to do something that would upset her. She kept waiting for him to out with it, but instead he continued to leave her wondering.

They had hurried out of the house and to the waiting black cab. The driver loaded Violet's case and then maneuvered the auto through the crowded streets. They were close enough to make the train if nothing interfered, which only left them worrying rather than leaning back to relax. Jack's knee was bouncing as he glanced at his pocket watch before looking out the window. His shoulders were tense, and he leaned forward as though he could will the autos in front of them to clear the way.

Violet felt certain that Jack would have shrugged off missing their intended train if they hadn't been traveling with his good friend, Hamilton Barnes.

During the war, Jack had worked with Mr. Barnes investigating crimes committed within the military ranks. When they'd come home, Mr. Barnes had pulled Jack into Scotland Yard when cases came that involved former military men. As Jack's experience grew and his brilliance at investigating became apparent to more than only Barnes, Jack was asked in on more and more cases. These days, Jack was investigating as often as not.

It was for Mr. Barnes that they were traveling to Oxford. He had written a recent journal article about modern investigative techniques and the application of recent learnings in science. He had invited them to the lecture along with a dinner and reception in his honor.

It was a hot summer's day, and between comforting Ginny and dressing in a hurry, Violet was boiling. She had selected a pale pink sailor's dress with cream accents and a drop waist. It was particularly loose on her, so she hoped it would cool her off. So far her hopes were being dashed again and again. She fanned herself with papers from her bag, fairly certain they were the first few pages of the manuscript Victor had sent with her to look over, but at the moment, they were the reason she hadn't fainted from the heat.

"What happened?" Jack asked as they left the auto. He took both of their cases and hurried ahead before Vi could answer, worried more about getting on the train than an immediate answer, she was sure. She followed after those broad shoulders, keeping easy track of him in the crowd. They already had their tickets, so all they had to do was make it to the train. The whistle was blowing as they ran, but Jack's massive form seemed to part the seas of the crowd as they ran, with Violet's much smaller one following in his wake. Jack leapt onto the train, turning to help her, but she was already standing behind him. She gave him a cheeky grin, and he shook his head.

"I forget sometimes that you aren't the flower your name proclaims."

She winked at him. "Jack, darling, I have a twin brother. I have spent the entirety of my life either chasing or running faster than blokes like you. Though I will say that your long shanks increase the challenge."

He snorted and rolled his eye as the train rolled away from the station.

Even though Violet was tall for a woman, with Jack a few steps above her she'd gone from feeling delicate to downright childlike. She was slim, which made her seem longer, especially with her sharp features. She had dark coloring, clever eyes, and a lively expression that leant additional charm to already pretty features.

Jack, however, was a hulk of a man. He was taller than most, broader than most, and quite muscular. With those penetrating eyes, he could be alarming for the average person. As for Violet, he generally made her feel both safe and cherished. It helped that he had made it clear he loved her, both with his words and even more with his actions. It was apparent in the way he put her happiness at the forefront of his personal concerns. The fact that Jack was an honorable man was even more comforting. She could entirely trust his word when he declared his love.

She'd had to defend his character more than once. Too often, people claimed that Jack pursued her only for her status as an earl's daughter or for her recent inheritance. Violet's stepmother hated that Jack worked, and liked to mention variations of the scoundrel that Jack must be in every letter.

"We made it," Violet pronounced rather unnecessarily. "What a promising beginning to a couple of days! Though you should be warned that tomorrow I intend to let you do all the work on the water. I will simply fan myself, adjust my hat, and trail my fingers in the river. It will be a good contrast, since I was forced to race to the train today. Keeping you and me in good form and all that."

"I think that means," Jack said, as he pulled her into the train carriage, "that you will have to carry the conversation during the gathering after Ham's speech. Perhaps something like, 'Oh, the wicked weather.'" Jack grinned as he added, "'What a lovely dress, Miss So-and-so! Did you get it in Paris? My brother and I were thinking of acquiring some chocolate liqueur and a new wardrobe. I *do* need a fancy dress for that party Algie is having.' Or other inanities that pass for conversation."

This holiday version of Jack startled Violet, reminding her of his teasing during their recent trip to Cuba.

"Don't be absurd," Violet said dryly. "Algie would never throw a party that he had to pay for."

Jack laughed, and then his head tilted as he examined her. "It is hot."

"Wickedly hot," Violet agreed, using his word. "My new favorite way of describing the weather." She fanned herself. "I've wilted."

She must be horrifically red for him to comment on the heat. She dug out her handkerchief and dabbed at her forehead. Any remnants of her powder had to have already disappeared.

"Shall we find Ham, take a seat, and dream of ices?" He knew she'd assent, so he closed the carriage door and led the way down the aisle, blocking Violet's view of anything ahead with those shoulders.

"Oh!" Longing filled Violet's voice. "A lemon one. Or ice cream. Or the both. I like to mix them."

"You are spoiled, my darling. Two treats mixed together?" His voice changed as he finished the final word, and Violet felt a flare of concern.

"Em?" he choked out. "Is that you?"

Em? Violet bit the inside of her mouth to keep a composed expression, which was immediately challenged by the lilting voice that replied.

"Jack! How lovely."

There was the sound of shuffling, and Violet pushed a little on Jack's wide back so she could see. As he stepped to the side at her prodding, Violet found a simply dazzling woman sitting next to Mr. Barnes. He was sitting near a window—a rotund man with a bald head, sharp eyes, and a suit that had seen better days. Next to the woman, he seemed all the more plebeian.

It was the way her features were framed that made her shockingly lovely. She was lush with golden brown hair, lovely golden brown eyes, full lips, and peaches and cream skin. Violet hesitated, feeling an unwelcome flash of jealousy that intensified as the woman—this Em—stepped into Jack's space and pressed a kiss on his cheek, leaving behind a smear of red lipstick. Violet found her gaze frozen on the mark. Those perfect lush lips had left behind a mark on her Jack. *Her* Jack.

Jack turned to Violet, his expression smooth as he held out his hand. She put her hand into his and let him draw her close. "Emily, may I present my very dear friend, Lady Violet Carlyle? Vi, this is an old acquaintance of mine, Miss Emily Allen. It is still Miss, isn't it?"

"I find myself ill-inclined to retire that form of address, Jack. You know that." Her expression was fraught with meaning, but Violet refused to let self-doubt creep in. The woman turned to Violet. "We were engaged to be married once. I'm afraid it all came to naught. To be honest, sometimes I wonder what it would be like to be Mrs. James Wakefield. No doubt there would be little ones running around and summers spent by the sea."

"Perhaps," Jack said quellingly. He pulled Violet's hand into the crook of his elbow, allowing her claim on him in the face of those musings.

"Jack," Violet said lightly, "you would be tortured by little girls, I think. If ever I have seen a man who will melt for a child with his own eyes, it's this one. I, on the other hand, am melting in this heat. Such a wicked hot day, isn't it?" Violet winked at Jack, who didn't miss her reference from moments ago. "Hullo, Mr. Barnes. So happy to see you. And to see you saved us a spot on this rolling oven. It's all my fault we're late, I swear. Jack was innocently delayed by my own naughty self."

Behind her bright chatter, Violet was grateful for her earlier thoughts about Jack's honor. If those ideas hadn't been at the forefront of her mind, she may well have transformed into a jealous ninny, shooting evil glances at the man she loved. With a man like Jack, she reminded herself, there was no question that he was honorable. As such, there was also no question that whoever this woman was, she was his past. Nothing more.

Violet and Jack might not be officially linked, but she was certain that when he envisioned those little ones in the future, she was their mother.

Violet smiled to Mr. Barnes, who was sweating in his corded jacket.

"Oh, Mr. Barnes. I feel certain you will expire on this train before we reach Oxford. Do loosen your tie and perhaps remove that jacket. I promise I will never, ever tell my stepmother or anyone else who would object."

"The Countess?" Miss Allen inquired.

Violet smirked and nodded, waving her face with the pages from the start of the manuscript. "The most stringent of women for *propriety*, I'm afraid."

"Then she must not be thrilled by you traveling with your

gentleman friend to Oxford," Miss Allen said, with enough acerbic tone to imply improprieties without stating them aloud.

Violet said nothing at the accusation. She wasn't going to defend herself to someone stupid enough to break off with Jack and then be tart with Violet because she wasn't as dim-witted. Violet was well-aware that the expression in this woman's gaze was envy. "Tell me, Mr. Barnes, are you quaking with nervousness?"

Mr. Barnes loosened his tie and removed his jacket. He probably wouldn't have, Vi thought, without Miss Allen's comment. In taking off the jacket, he was moving the conversation from whatever improprieties Jack and Violet might have been indulging in. Violet inclined her head to Mr. Barnes, knowing he'd follow her thoughts. Like Jack, Mr. Barnes was almost supernatural in his understanding of the human beast and the environment around them.

"Ham? Nervous?" Miss Allen laughed, but they were all aware she'd used the pet-name for Mr. Barnes simply to elucidate her status versus Violet's. Miss Allen, unlike Violet, was on a first-name basis with Mr. Barnes. Vi ignored the implication, keeping her cheery smile in place.

"Nervous?" Mr. Barnes repeated with a shrug. "Perhaps a bit. The fellows who will be at this presentation are all about language and theory. The realities are far different, don't you know? Especially when dealing with witnesses who lie or criminals actively working against the police force. It's much easier to solve the crimes humanity commits on each other based off of theories than realities."

Violet nodded, as did Miss Allen. The woman seemed to know exactly what he was talking about. Just what experience did she have? Was she a female police officer? But no...not on a first-class carriage in those custom clothes.

Mr. Barnes continued. "That's what makes someone like Jack so valuable. He knows and understands the theories, but he also has vast experience with the vagaries of humanity. These Oxford boys, they judge the in-field fellows like Jack or my inspectors without ever understanding what's it like walking into a crime scene, taking it all in, and finding the relevant clues while disregarding the irrelevant. You, my dear, are an excellent example. You have more—unfortunate and undesirable—but very real experience than those who will be attending this lecture. You will, I think, get even more from it than they, though I hope you will never find yourself using it again."

"As do I." For a moment, Vi forgot they had an audience. "You know, Victor and I are near fighting over our next book. I wonder if we shouldn't set aside the plans each of us has and write something rather full of detectives and spies and what did you call it? Ah yes. The vagaries of human nature."

Mr. Barnes laughed, as Miss Allen's head cocked. With her gaze fixed on Violet's makeshift fan, Miss Allen asked, "Write? Are you a writer?"

CHAPTER TWO

*V*iolet lied through her smile. "Who doesn't enjoy playing with words? My brother and I have been telling each other stories since we were in short-pants. Terrifying tales to horrify our poor nanny."

She glanced at Jack, setting the pages of the manuscript face down on her lap in what Vi hoped was a casual manner.

He immediately tried to sidetrack Miss Allen from Violet's blunder. "Ham, did you read the conclusion of the strangler case near Chinatown?"

"Nasty business," Hamilton said. "One of my best men worked on that one and nearly got side-tracked a time or two. This is what I'm talking about, Lady Carlyle. All the learning in the world, all the experience you could possibly have, and you still find yourself derailed by the humans who are fighting against you. They are fighting, you know? Fighting to keep you from finding out what they've done. Struggling to..."

Violet stopped listening. Miss Allen's gaze was fixed on Violet's face, and there was enough of a smirk that Violet felt certain the woman was nearly as clever as Jack and Hamilton. Violet's blunder might have revealed her and Victor's hidden identity as V. V. Twinnings, author of the fantastical and ridiculous. Especially with their pseudonym and title of the current work on the cover page, resting face down in Violet's lap.

The best she could do to excuse herself was to blame being off-her-game with Miss Emily Allen, Jack's former betrothed, sitting across from her like a horror-filled phantasm.

Violet loved a good pulp novel. The Tarzan books, the Bulldog Drummond books, even the old Varney the Vampire. They were so fun in their intent to be nothing more than a way to pass an afternoon.

Her stepmother, however—what would she say if she found out Violet and Victor had supplemented their allowance with writing books that she didn't even want them reading? What would Father say?

"You know," Miss Allen said, in the lull in the conversation. "I also like to play with words. I'm a reporter for the Piccadilly Press. I find that when one wields the pen, women can be equals, don't you think?"

Violet shrugged as though she weren't panicking at the realization that this woman *wrote* about people like Violet for a living. The Piccadilly Press *loved* stories about the rich and well-connected. And Violet had exposed her status as an author. Both hers and Victor's.

With an even expression, she said, "There's a reason that Miss Evans published under George Eliot and the Brontës under Bell. One would hope that with our fight for equal rights, we will eventually see women who only write with a man's name because they wish to and not because they feel the need to do so in order for their work to be received. Perhaps even the day will come when a man will choose to use a woman's name for the same reasons women currently use men's names. Some genre that they wish to write in that is dominated by female writers. What a lovely fantasy!"

Neither Jack nor Hamilton laughed, but Miss Allen did. She lifted a condescending brow. "I don't approve of women pretending to be men to create a career. Better instead to be a pioneer for the women who follow."

Violet didn't agree, but she didn't wish to get into a debate. Not every decision needed to be made simply to forge the path for those who came behind. Sometimes a woman—or a man— needed to make their choices based upon what was best for them and what was right for them, despite the larger implications.

Violet crossed her ankles and noted the passing scenery. Thankfully the journey wasn't all that long. Perhaps she and Jack could find a shady spot to cool off when they arrived? She felt after the fraught conversation and morning, she could use some time in the open air before they went to a stifling lecture hall, let alone having to dress for Hamilton's lecture. She could only hope that the ceilings were high, they had fans near every window, and that the hall wasn't too crowded.

"Been receiving a rather odd series of letters from one of the lads at Oxford. He's been making claims about a possible murder," Mr. Barnes told Jack as they neared the town. "I should have you take a look at them later today if there's time. I was thinking of looking up the boy tomorrow. Do you have plans?"

"Indeed, I have promised Violet some time on the water," Jack started.

"A promise I am physically incapable of rescinding," Violet told Hamilton. "In this heat, I may need to trail my fingers in the water or expire."

"I'd be happy, however," Jack continued, "to look at the letters with you, Ham. What's so odd about them?"

"Better to see for yourself," Mr. Barnes replied. "Be nice to get a set of fresh eyes on them and see if I'm seeing ghosts where there are only shadows. Too much time amidst crimes, you know, and suddenly every statement is a lie and every passerby a criminal."

"Oh, Mr. Barnes." Violet reached out and touched his wrist lightly. "You must focus on the good men in your work, those like Jack who are honorable, to find your hope. Otherwise you shall be very grim indeed. Perhaps you should take some time off. A little time on the Amalfi Coast? Or Cuba! Don't you think Cuba, Jack?"

"Not everyone is delighted by odd flavors, sandy shores, and rum cocktails as you and Victor," Jack told her. "I think our Ham here would like nothing more than a few weeks in his childhood home. He grew up near your father's estate. Did you know?"

"Did you?" Violet asked. "Did you really?"

"Used to see your brothers gallivanting about quite often, to be honest," he said.

When Violet's grin dimmed, it was Mr. Barnes who touched her wrist. "We are the worse for their loss, Lady Vi. Very much the worse. I am sorry. I shouldn't have..."

She shook her head, blinking her eyes rapidly. "I think you simply caught me unaware, dear Mr. Barnes. I did lose greatly in the war, as did we all. It warms my heart to know that it is not only those of us who were related to them who miss Lionel and Peter and regret their loss."

"Heard of your Lionel during the war, actually," Mr. Barnes said. "Never wanted to bring it up to you given...well...he was a good man, Lady Violet. A truly good man. He died a hero and was loved by those who served with him."

Violet was blinking even more rapidly as the train rolled to a stop. None of them moved. The aisles would be crowded, and it was often better to let those passengers in a rush leave first and follow at a more reasonable pace.

"Tell me, Lady Carlyle," Miss Allen said, after the first rush of passengers left. "What do you do when you aren't following Jack about the country?"

"Oh, all the normal things," Violet lied, noting the glint in Miss Allen's gaze. This woman probably saw right through Vi's lie, which was downright astounding. Violet had lied her way through many an uncomfortable situation without being caught, and this woman seemed to sense every single half-truth. "Fancy dress parties, shopping, naps, treasure hunts."

Those were all activities that Violet actually did and did often. The bulk of her time, however, was spent writing with her twin, with random good works, managing her late aunt's business interests, and mentoring two young girls—one being Violet's actual ward. How many bright young things were raising a former street urchin or looking after a fortune as Violet did? She already knew the answer—none of them.

Many of her generation were brilliant, but Vi was well aware that there were far more layabouts than stalwarts.

"Shall we then?" Jack said, standing to take down the cases for himself and Violet. Mr. Barnes followed a moment later.

"We'll be seeing you, Emily," the older man said.

"This evening," she told him in a merry voice. "I was sent down to cover your lecture for one of the boys who can't make it tonight, Ham. His mother or sister or second-cousin is ill and when they discovered I actually knew you, well, I was the obvious choice. I'll spend the afternoon with my brother and join you all for the evening." Miss Allen's gaze darted over Violet, and her smile was a cool, snake's smile. "Lady Carlyle, a pleasure. Gentlemen." She took her case from Mr. Barnes and disappeared after the others.

Violet blew out her breath in a rush. "I've spoiled things, haven't I?"

"Your books aren't anything to be ashamed of, Vi." Jack's voice was careful, which told Violet that yes, she had exposed herself and her twin.

Mr. Barnes shot her a commiserating look. "We can hope that she'll be kind." Violet lifted a brow, and Mr. Barnes's expression shifted. "Well, perhaps not. She was rather territorial even after... well...it doesn't help that you're with Jack."

"I suppose Victor will forgive me. Perhaps I shall hunt up some sort of magical liqueur or wine or other concoction to bolster him before the *countess* descends on us. Wrath of the mighty et cetera, et cetera. One should quake in advance of what is to come."

"Warning your brother is, I think, an excellent plan," Mr. Barnes said gently. He stepped back so that Violet could proceed him.

Jack paused, still facing her, and searched her face. "Will it be all right?"

Violet nodded, though she was upset. Victor would forgive her. The books were frivolous but not scandalous, so Jack was right in that she didn't have to be ashamed of them. That didn't mean her stepmother wouldn't both shame Violet and refuse to forgive the twins.

Violet had long felt a day of accounting coming for herself with her stepmother. The best hope she could find was that she had time to formulate her thoughts before her stepmother attacked. No doubt, she'd move far beyond the books to every-thing that had ever bothered her, whether they'd discussed it previously or not.

Jack led the way off the train. His broad shoulders parted the crowd again, and Violet and Mr. Barnes traveled in his wake.

They all had small suitcases, so they decided to walk to their lodgings rather than suffer through another stifling journey in an auto.

As they moved through the streets, Violet pulled both men to a stop. "What magical mirage is this? Can it be? Is it so?"

Jack followed Violet's gaze. With a laugh, the three of them changed course and found a table near a window. They ordered their lemon ices. Violet made both men order a scoop of ice cream as well. The mix of the flavors had Mr. Barnes sighing and Jack scrunching his nose and shaking his head.

"You are broken inside," Violet told him. Mr. Barnes agreed. She smiled down at her half-melted remnants. "I suppose that these are rather indulgent."

"Indeed," Jack told her with the smallest of smirks.

She wasn't repentant and wasn't going to be repentant, so she simply grinned and handed him the last of her ice cream. He finished it off in one large bite, and they rose to continue to the house of Mr. Daniel Morgan.

CHAPTER THREE

*T*hey were to stay with Mr. Morgan while in Oxford. As a long-time friend of both Jack and Mr. Barnes, Mr. Morgan had arranged the lecture, dinner, and reception. Mr. Morgan was a professor at Oxford but spent much of his time researching. He had several assistants who stayed in Oxford over the summer holidays to help with his research projects.

Jack explained that the students fought for that honor, and Violet admitted to surprise. She'd enjoyed her time at university, but she'd enjoyed her holidays too much to stay behind and keep working. She had never been focused on school to the point of missing her holidays.

Mr. Morgan wasn't in attendance when they arrived at his home, but they'd known that would be the case. His butler, however, was in attendance and ready to show them to their rooms. Violet immediately freshened up with a cool bath that left her a new woman. With the cooler evening air, she just might make it through the day.

Violet explored after her bath but before she actually dressed for the evening, noting the large room for the reception already had fans running in each of the windows. With any luck, the room would be chilled by the time they returned from the lecture to enjoy the dinner that Mr. Morgan's staff were preparing.

The library was stocked to the extreme, with books sitting on tables and bulging off the shelves, and stacks of books in front of the shelved ones. It seemed that Mr. Morgan could use a library at least twice the size.

She walked through the house, noting pictures on the walls, with what looked like students from years previous, alongside a man, who Violet assumed was Mr. Morgan himself. In several of the photos and even a painting, he stood with a young woman who looked to be around the age of Violet's younger sister.

Violet hadn't heard Jack or Mr. Barnes speak of the girl. Was she a daughter? A friend? Perhaps connected in some other way? Perhaps she wouldn't be at the house, so they hadn't seen any need to mention her.

Violet returned to her room when the clock rang out, telling her she'd better hurry or she'd be late. She was determined to be on time for the rest of this trip and in the future until the guilt of nearly missing the train had fully faded.

For the hot evening in a lecture hall, Violet chose a sleeveless black dress with a drop waist, fringy hem, and a long strand of turquoise beads that Victor had acquired for her in Cuba. She wore T-strap shoes with diamond buckles and draped a sheer black wrap around her shoulders.

She faced herself in the mirror after her makeup was perfected, but was distracted by thoughts of the young woman from the portraits. Her dress and bob proclaimed her a woman of Violet's generation. Who could the woman be? She was well-aware, through Jack, that Mr. Morgan was a bachelor. This girl couldn't be his child, could she? Perhaps she was a ward, like

Violet's Ginny? Or the daughter of a friend? Violet supposed that the girl could be cousin or niece.

Whatever her connection, she was truly lovely. She had golden blonde hair, bright blue eyes, and a dimple in her chin. The artist had caught a lively glint in her eyes and a smile at the edges of her mouth that said this was a woman who was ready for a dance and a joke. Violet felt certain she'd like the woman should she ever have a chance to meet her.

She checked her watch and hurried from her room to make her way down the stairs. Her goal to be early had been successful, and she descended a good ten minutes before they'd agreed to leave. She tried to hide her flash of frustration when she found Jack and the man from the photographs waiting for her.

"Just in time," Jack told her.

"I am ten minutes early, I'll have you know. At least, I would have been if you weren't so abominably obsessed with punctuality." She said it with a laugh.

Jack held out his hand and introduced her to an older man with large sideburns and rather delightful eyebrows. They were so dominant that they commanded his whole face, accentuating each expression dramatically. She hadn't noticed them in the photos, but she supposed that was because they weren't moving around as if they had a life of their own.

"Daniel Morgan, my dear. It's a pleasure to meet you."

"And you." Violet grinned at him and his eyes flicked over her, taking her in and glinting with approval.

"Come my friends," Jack said. "We cannot be late for Ham."

Violet placed her hand on Jack's arm, and they made their way to the lecture. The lecture hall was close to Mr. Morgan's house. Jack whispered to Violet about his days at school as they passed through the green and along the walks. The sun was yet up, but the shadows were lengthening.

The evening had cooled enough that Violet didn't feel as though she'd sweat off her makeup, and she enjoyed the breeze and the conversation between the two men, who were clearly long-time friends. As they spoke, they referenced events that had happened long before, during the war and after, as they'd come home to the changed world.

Violet had never considered what it must have been like to return from the war. She and Victor both had only suffered in the periphery. Victor had been too young to serve until the final year, and then only started his training, becoming injured, and the war ending while he'd been recovering.

For Jack though—he'd grown up before the war, served from the first, seen terrible things, and come back to a world that must have been different in every aspect from his early years. How had she not considered that before? Violet had seen her friend, Tomas, suffer, but Jack didn't carry his service in shuddering memories and waking nightmares as Tomas did. At least, she hadn't witnessed anything of the sort.

She was horrified by her lack of imagination. Did Jack care that she hadn't realized? Or did he appreciate that she didn't see his ghosts?

She shook the thoughts off as they arrived at the lecture hall. It was far more crowded than Violet had expected, and given some of the fellows sitting around, it wasn't only the intellectual, professorial types here. Many of these lads had to be students. It was the summer. Were there truly this many students doing summer research? Some of the others were clearly police officers. Maybe they wanted to rise through the ranks? The mix of atten-dees was rather surprising.

A student greeted Mr. Morgan as they arrived and led them to their seats. Mr. Barnes was near the podium, speaking with several other men, but he nodded slightly to Jack and Mr.

Morgan before returning his attention to the men in front of him.

"Mr. Wakefield?"

Jack faced the young man, who held out his hand. "I'm Jeremiah Allen. Perhaps you remember me?"

Jack jerked, startled, before studying the young man. "By Jove, Jeremy! Of course I do. I thought you looked familiar."

Allen? Violet examined the lad and didn't see much if any link between him and the Miss Allen. Were they related? What were the chances? Hadn't Miss Allen referred to her brother? Though she'd been distracted by her blunder, Violet felt certain that Miss Allen had before she sauntered off the train.

The young man grinned delightedly. "I'm a huge fan, sir. Just a huge fan. Always have been really. Mr. Morgan asked me to show people to their seats. Yours are right this way. It is so nice to see you again."

The nervous, excited chatter from the young man made Violet smile, though she worked to hide the expression. To this young man, Jack was a hero. Violet felt the young Mr. Allen had excellent taste.

She saw the pure pleasure in Jack's gaze at seeing this man again. "None of that 'sir' nonsense. I believe you once called me Jack. It would be welcome once again."

Jack, Mr. Morgan, and Violet followed the young man. He stuttered an assent before he gushed. "I read your article last month. It was just...just..."

Violet didn't hide her grin as Jack's cheeks tinged the slightest bit red. A person would have to know him fairly well to realize he was embarrassed. The young man had to have been only in his first couple of years of schooling, though maybe she thought so because he was baby-faced. His face was round with full lips, big brown eyes, and slick backed hair. There was too much vigor in those golden brown locks for a pomade to be effective, but he was valiantly attempting the style of the day.

Like Jack, Jeremiah Allen was a large man, though he had yet to come fully into his potential size. He was more the shadow of what was to come. He didn't look much like his sister, if indeed she was. She was femininity personified. However, they did have the same color of eyes. They both had those full lips. They both had the same peaches and cream skin, probably far less desirable for the brother than the sister.

"I've been conducting some experiments. Have you read Dr. Thorpe's essay on decomposing flesh?"

Violet shuddered, and Jack shot her a grin. "I have indeed. May I introduce my friend, Lady Violet Carlyle?"

Mr. Allen hadn't seemed to even notice her before Jack introduced them, and when Mr. Allen turned his attention to her, his cheerful gaze faded. His gazed narrowed as he said, "Mr. Wakefield, I...Em...oh..." Mr. Allen flushed, nodded once, and said, "I believe I'm supposed to be seating others. An usher, don't you know?" He fled before they could reply.

Violet watched the young man retreat. He'd known something about his sister, for there was no doubt now that Miss Allen was that. Was Miss Allen bemoaning that she'd lost Jack? Had she disparaged Violet to Mr. Allen?

"What the devil is wrong with that boy?" Mr. Morgan asked, turning to stare after Mr. Allen with eyebrows aiming down like furious arrows. "Unacceptable way to treat Lady Violet. He's one of my lads, just added when another left me. Not sure I made the best choice there, but he was so enthusiastic. Worked as a general servant boy for whatever we needed for months before the last of my lads left. He already knew...anyhow. I apologize, Lady Violet."

"It's of little matter, Mr. Morgan. Cheer up, turn those

eyebrows upside down." She winked at him when he cast her a startled glance and then burst into a guffaw.

When he'd gathered himself, he told Jack, "I like this one so much more."

Violet caught the 'more,' but she didn't let her expression alter. She also caught the glance from Jack but carefully avoided his gaze.

The seats that had been reserved for them were at the front, and Mr. Barnes walked over to shake hands with Jack and Mr. Morgan just as a tall, slim man stepped up to the podium and gathered the attention of the attendees. Mr. Barnes kissed Violet's cheek before returning to his seat as his introduction began.

Violet had known that Jack and Mr. Barnes had been compatriots during the war but not the honors that Mr. Barnes had attained. She hadn't been aware of his degree from the university or the well-known cases that he had solved. In the end, she'd only known that Jack loved the man like a brother and that he was one of the few men that Jack held in true esteem.

Violet had intended to pay close attention to Mr. Barnes's speech, but her mind was caught in the 'more' of Mr. Morgan's comment. He had been, of course, referring to Miss Allen and supposedly liking Violet more. How could he come to that conclusion after a short walk unless Jack had been talking to him about Violet? Unless he'd generally despised Miss Allen. Jack and Miss Allen had been betrothed and all his friends here had known her well. There was history there, Violet thought, and rather a lot of it. How did she feel about it?

She reminded herself that Jack was older than she. Even Violet had romantic associations before Jack, but he'd been the only one who had captured her heart. He had no reason to be jealous of those who'd come before him, and the same should apply to her even if he'd been betrothed while she hadn't.

With her eyes fixed on Mr. Barnes, Violet wondered what had happened between Miss Allen and Jack. Violet could feel Jack's gaze on her here and there. Each time, he returned his attention to his friend before Violet met his eyes. She tilted her head and pretended to listen, but she wasn't interested in the efficacy of fingerprints or the ways to detect poison. Those sciences could be betrayed, and she'd meddled in enough of Jack's previous cases to feel that it was the person who was of most intrigue. Violet had no intention of getting fingerprinting powder and a magnifying glass or putting on the hat of a bobbie.

She wouldn't have normally come with Jack to this type of event. She'd been persuaded by the idea of a day on the water. Maybe she should consider a few weeks by the sea? Violet wondered if Jack would join them. Maybe if she and Victor took their ward, Ginny, it would be reason enough for Kate to be able to escape her mother and rejoin them as well. She was, after all, engaged to Victor. The time for Mrs. Lancaster to loosen her hold on her daughter had long since come and gone.

Violet's attention was distracted from her inner-monologue with a whispered argument behind her. Jack was slowly stiffening as people glanced their way, but the villains were seated almost directly behind them. Vi slipped her hand into Jack's jacket pocket, took his handkerchief, and dropped it.

As she leaned down to pick it up, she spied Jeremiah Allen arguing with two other students and his sister. As they hissed back and forth, Miss Allen silenced her brother with a sharp elbow to the ribs, a smooth smile on her face and every hair in place. The cold look she still managed to shoot his companions snapped their mouths closed.

Violet sat upright, glancing at Jack out of the corner of her eye, and caught his half-smirk as she handed him back his hand-kerchief. She took her fan from her handbag——an actual fan this time——and waved it on both of them as Mr. Barnes carried on without reflecting an ounce of distraction by the young fools seated behind them.

The lecture ended, and with it, Violet and Jack rose to congratulate Mr. Barnes on quite an absorbing talk. It was all lies on Violet's part, given she hadn't really listened, and Mr. Barnes was quite observant enough to know she was giving him idle compliments, but he grinned as she waxed on. She finally sput-tered to an end with a rather pathetic slew of adjectives, to his clear amusement.

Mr. Allen, however, picked up where Violet petered out. His companions hadn't elbowed their way forward as the young man had. They were watching from the sidelines, shooting him rather alarming looks as they hissed back and forth.

They came to a quick stop in their argument when Mr. Morgan approached them. His eyebrows were ferociously down-turned and whatever he said had both of the students paling, nodding frantically, and making their way to the rear of the lecture hall.

CHAPTER FOUR

*V*iolet excused herself to the powder room, and when she approached the mirror she found Miss Allen waiting, leaning against a table that had been set up for the ladies to check their makeup or freshen their hair.

"I was hoping I'd have a chance to speak with you." Miss Allen smiled smoothly, without the expression ever reaching those golden brown orbs. "Just us girls."

Ominous, Violet thought, but she remained outwardly unruffled as though she didn't feel hunted. How odd it was to be tracked down by the woman that Jack had once wanted to *marry*. Violet opened her handbag and pulled out her lipstick. With a precise hand, she applied the red lip, blotted it, and repeated the measure. She touched up her powder next, all the while waiting for Miss Allen to speak.

"I was hoping for a favor," Miss Allen said, with those cold brown eyes fixed on Violet's naked ring finger, as she ran a brush through her hair and replaced her headpiece.

Violet lifted a brow, meeting those honey eyes with her own dark ones. She straightened her strand of turquoise beads and smoothed the fringe of her dress, waiting silently for Miss Allen to expand on that startling statement.

Miss Allen seemed to give up on making Violet reply. It had been a ploy to make Violet open herself up, and Vi was far beyond those kind of games.

"My brother Jeremiah seems to have need...perhaps need is too strong of a word. He requires assistance. If Jack could step in..." Miss Allen trailed off, either unwilling to continue or attempting to prompt a response from Violet.

Violet relented. "With the university?"

"With Jeremy's professors. Look, Jack might not seem like it, but he's a bit of a brainy fellow and he's kept friendly with these types. That Mr. Morgan for instance. Jeremy has wanted to be just like Jack since he and I were...intended. Jeremy needs help. He's made a blunder of things and doesn't even see it. He keeps bullishly pushing ahead, ruining his life."

"Jack is who you need to ask about this, Miss Allen." Violet clicked her handbag closed.

"He'll say no." There was no doubt in Miss Allen's voice. "Jeremy's theory about the murder of some girl is ridiculous."

"No? To a boy he once mentored?" Violet didn't think so, but she wouldn't be making any promises for Jack. "As you know, Jack Wakefield—"

"Will do anything for the woman he loves. I know that better than anyone—" Miss Allen's eyes drifted over Violet's face, and then the woman begrudgingly added, "except perhaps for yourself."

"You'll still need to ask Jack. I am not his secretary nor am I his conscience." Violet spun on her heel. "A pleasure, Miss Allen."

Violet started to open the door when Miss Allen smoothly said, "I figured it out, you know. V.V. Twinnings. It's not really that clever, is it?"

Violet closed her eyes. She could hear her stepmother's diatribe as if she were hearing an echo from the future. Something so horrible it rebounded both ways through time.

Violet opened the door and left without replying. She stepped outside of the lecture hall for a few minutes to recover her temper before she returned to Jack's side.

Of all the cheek! Did Miss Allen truly believe that she could just...just...force Violet—and through Violet, Jack—to do the bidding of the harridan? And Jack had loved that woman? Loved her enough to marry her? Had those penetrating eyes of his been blinded? He'd actually dreamed of children with her someday? Violet's only hope was that the woman had changed dramatically since Jack had thought to wed her.

When she returned to the lecture hall, she found Miss Allen standing next to Jack with her hand on his arm. Violet paused, staring at the group. They seemed to know each other quite well. Not one of the people gathered were reacting to seeing the two together. Miss Allen was standing rather too close to Jack for Violet's liking, but Violet would be damned if she'd allow the woman to play Violet like an instrument.

Violet approached and heard one of the men say, "I wondered if you'd be here, Jack. It has been too long." They shook hands heartily and then the fellow nodded to Miss Allen and said, "Lovely as always, Em. Saw your brother running about."

One of the other men snorted and a couple of them shot him a sharp glance. Violet noted the interaction, as did Miss Allen, who flushed lightly.

Mr. Barnes saw Violet and stepped back enough to give her

space next to him. She stepped into the circle, placing her hand on his arm, and saw Jack focus on that hand. It was all rather untenable, wasn't it? Miss Allen was using his manners against him and Violet's secrets against herself and her twin. Miss Allen worming her way into their relationships, especially with whatever had been bothering Jack hanging over the both of them.

"Have you met Miss Allen?" Mr. Morgan asked Violet a few minutes later, when the conversation allowed. His eyebrows maneuvered about his face as though he seemed to expect Violet to fall into semi-hysterics to see Jack with his former-betrothed.

"Indeed," Violet told him. "I feel I am discovering her nature with each passing moment."

Jack and Miss Allen both shot Violet sharp glances, but Mr. Morgan simply shuffled those epic eyebrows about his face and introduced Violet to the rest of the company before anyone descended into a catfight. The fellows returned to the investigative techniques, and Violet let her mind wander.

"We're probably boring you," Mr. Morgan said a few minutes later, when Violet glanced over her shoulder.

"Lady Carlyle is rather too clever when it comes to such things. Don't be distracted by her bright eyes. She's got a wicked wit as well," Mr. Barnes told the others. "If she's bored, it's because she isn't hearing anything new."

"You're pouring it on rather thickly, Mr. Barnes," she told him. "I will have to deflate my ego before I am able to return home, should you keep these unwarranted compliments up."

Mr. Barnes squeezed her fingers and laughed heartily. He changed the subject, but a few minutes later, Miss Allen took the attention to herself. She commented on his speech and inquired into one of his recent cases. It was clear that Miss Allen knew what she was speaking of and had come prepared. Her lashes fluttered as she tried to charm Mr. Barnes. Violet hadn't been paying much attention to the cases that Mr. Barnes was working or any of the cases that had ended up in Jack's lap, but she saw Miss Allen's compliments for what they were. She was using her wiles on Mr. Barnes to get quotes for her article.

They chatted for several minutes and the circle around Mr. Barnes thinned as people said their good-byes. They were left with Jack, Miss Allen on his arm, and Violet, her hand on the crook of Mr. Barnes's elbow. Mr. Morgan was standing between the two couples, his gaze focused on the students who had lingered.

"It's been a while, Emily," Mr. Morgan said. "I didn't expect you to come."

She smiled prettily. "I'm here as a sister and for the Piccadilly Press. Have you met my brother, Jeremiah Allen? He says he's been in some of your lectures."

"Ah, yes."

"He waxes on and on about you," Miss Allen told Mr. Morgan, who didn't seem to be flattered. When that compliment didn't work, she let go of Jack to place her hand on Mr. Morgan's arm. She leaned towards him, giving a rather full glimpse of her bosom. "Oh Daniel, I did want to convey my condolences about the loss of your niece. I...she...I liked her so much."

"Thank you," he said rather sharply, and turned to Mr. Barnes to change the subject.

Violet's interest was piqued, but she kept her expression even. Was this dead niece the young woman in the pictures and paintings Violet had seen? How had she died? The influenza? Something else? A terrible auto accident? Drowning? Illness?

Violet veiled her eyes as she reexamined the men and thought about Miss Allen. Vi had noted the first-name basis, which supported her idea that they all knew each other well. She felt very much like the odd duck out in a bevy of swans. But then again, those gents had been nice enough to Miss Allen, while Mr. Morgan hadn't softened when Miss Allen had started up with the womanly ploys.

In fact, none of them had. Mr. Barnes had seemed fully aware each time Miss Allen had complimented him. These were men who weren't beguiled by women—or at least by Miss Allen. What had her intentions been? Was she simply hoping they'd stumble into saying something valuable for her paper? Something for her to prove her worth against the person who had been intended to write this article?

As if reading Violet's mind, Mr. Morgan said, "I believe you normally cover more women's events, do you not?" He looked to Violet. "Miss Allen is a reporter."

"So, I've heard," Violet told him. "We were discussing on the train how I also enjoy writing and playing with words."

Miss Allen smiled that smooth, flirtatious smile as she eyed Mr. Morgan, but her tone was condescending as she said, "It is playing, isn't it, when one is blessed with quite an income? I believe our paper wrote about your inheritance. Quite scandalous, wasn't it?"

Violet didn't let her serene expression slip. "I'm afraid so."

"Nothing to do with Vi." Jack's tone was sharp, and Miss Allen's expression smoothed from carefully vicious into innocent as she glanced towards him.

"Life's but a walking shadow," Violet quoted, "a poor player that struts and frets his hour upon the stage and then is heard no more. It is a tale told by an idiot..." Violet shrugged to Miss Allen. "I think we're mostly playing at life. We pretend to be capable in our work, in our interactions, in our family. Sometimes we might surprise ourselves, but more often than not we're stumbling through our part, doing what is expected, and constantly fighting our true self. That lazy layabout we all have inside who wants nothing more than a bottle of wine, a sunny garden, and a hound at our feet."

"Perhaps for you as an earl's daughter," Miss Allen shot back. "As a mere commoner who had to scrape and struggle—"

"Come now, Emily," Mr. Barnes interrupted with a snort. "Your father is as rich as Croesus, and you work because you want to. The same with Jack, who, I know for a fact, stumbled through most of our early cases, discovering the killer more by pure, idiotic luck. I was certainly playacting this evening as I gave my speech, assuming confidence I can promise you I did not feel."

"So you always say when you talk about my early cases," Jack said, "and yet discover them I did. Perhaps it was simply unwitting brilliance?" Jack faced Miss Allen, ending the conversation with, "I believe we're supposed to hurry along to Morgan's for dinner. Shall we see you at the reception, Emily?"

"I'm planning on it." She eyed Violet and then left.

"Is that young fellow, Jeremiah Allen, related to Emily?" Mr. Barnes asked. "The one the boys were making low-level jibes about before Emily appeared?"

Jack nodded. "Quite a younger brother. I think the lad must be in his first year. I wouldn't have thought to see him here, to be honest."

"He got to me after my speech," Mr. Barnes said. "Cut-off several others and about chattered my ear off until Morgan moved him along. Seems an excitable lad. He was the one writing me those letters that concerned me. I didn't connect that he was Emily's brother. I shall have to look him up if you agree the letters are as odd as I think."

"He's been making enemies among the lads," Mr. Morgan said, as he began walking the direction Miss Allen took. "Prosing on with an assumption of expertise I can assure you he does not have. When you add in his age and the way he used our connection to worm himself into my group of assistants, well...he's burning more bridges than he realizes."

Mr. Barnes winced for Mr. Allen, as did Jack. Violet, however, wanted to see it all in action. What good fodder for her book if she decided to write a mystery.

That was a heartless thought, but she wasn't feeling particularly generous towards the Allens.

"Ah. Unfortunate for the boy." Jack held out his hand to Violet, who hesitated a moment before putting her hand in his, hating herself the moment she did. They, both Jack and Mr. Barnes, noted her hesitation. Oh! Those observant fellows! It was frustrating at times that Jack was as clever as he was.

Mr. Barnes stepped in to the rescue before the tension between Jack and Violet could ratchet up. "Now tell me, Violet, what is that brother of yours up to?"

"I assume you mean Victor and not the respectable Gerald?" She told Mr. Barnes the tale of Victor having sold the house he'd purchased while in his cups to another young fool, who had been drunkenly poetic over roses at their club. Victor, it seemed, knew men as rich and foolish as he, for he passed the house off sight-unseen on the description of the garden alone. The buyer was rich enough that Victor had been bragging he'd come out quite ahead in the deal, at least until Kate sat him down with a ledger and made him do the arithmetic.

They walked back to Mr. Morgan's house where the dinner party and reception would be held, and Violet noted how Jack kept glancing at her. She tried to give him a reassuring look, but she wasn't sure he bought it. Her silent scold continued, and she told herself that they were a young couple. She hadn't hesitated to take his hand because she was jealous. She'd hesitated because she wasn't sure she should tell Jack that his former betrothed was attempting to manipulate Violet into manipulating Jack. Vi felt quite sure that Jack would be enraged at the sheer idea.

CHAPTER FIVE

*A*s they walked towards Mr. Morgan's house, Mr. Barnes pulled ahead, drawing Mr. Morgan with him. It left Violet and Jack walking side-by-side with a measure of privacy. The sun had nearly set and the late dinner would be happening soon with an even later reception.

"Are you all right?" Jack's tone had that extra something in it that had been worrying her.

She nodded and smiled brightly. She wasn't ready to tell him of Miss Allen's manipulations. Not before Mr. Barnes's reception. Jack deserved to focus on his friend's successes, not worry about the nonsense Miss Allen was attempting.

"I know you lie with your smiles at times, Vi."

Violet licked her lips. "I was a bit surprised to discover her." Violet paused, searching her mind for a way to convey her feelings.

Before she could, Jack sighed. "I suppose I should have told you about her."

Violet lifted her brows and waited to see if he'd fill in the silence. She should have known better. He was the master of such games. She was playing them with him. Miss Allen was playing them with Violet. They were all too experienced with discovering truths to fall for such nonsenses.

"Did you expect to see her today?"

Jack shook his head.

"Then yes, eventually, you should have told me about her. But I am not angry that you were caught unawares. Would you have told me?"

"Yes. I suppose. She hasn't mattered for some time. I don't think about her anymore except to be glad that it all fell apart."

"Tell me about her now?" Violet asked.

Jack placed his hand over where her hand was on his arm. He played with her fingers as he admitted, "I loved her once."

She wasn't sure what to say, so she decided to err on the side of silence. Did it hurt to know he'd loved someone else? By heavens, yes. But she knew he loved her now, and she caught the 'once.' It was a relationship that had been before Violet. It had ended before Violet. She wasn't going to be a jealous ninny. She didn't need to be, even she knew that.

"She broke me for a while. I never intended to love again, Vi. I never expected to love like I love you. I didn't even realize what I felt for Em was a shadow of the possibilities of true loving."

Violet looked up at his face. "I didn't know I could be jealous." She only confessed it because they were being painfully honest, even if she hadn't allowed herself to admit it until that moment. "I didn't enjoy it."

"You don't have to be jealous when it comes to me, Vi. Not ever."

She squeezed his arm. "That goes for you as well."

He lifted her hand to his lips, pressed a kiss on the tips of her fingers, and then he nodded to the North Star. "Lovely evening despite everything. Did you know Ham gave me quite the scold?"

"With one fierce look?" Violet was sure that Mr. Barnes had done nothing more if he'd done even that.

"For Ham, he might as well have been shouting. He never liked Em. He loves you. Told me if you left me, he'd lose several stone and throw himself at your feet." Violet laughed as Jack lifted a brow. "He was serious, I think."

"You are both nonsensical," Violet told him, as they turned onto the street where they were staying. Mr. Morgan and Mr. Barnes were several houses ahead of the two of them, and Violet and Jack slowed even more.

"Time for inane chatter," Jack warned her.

"Mm. They'll all be trying to get you to tell them about your cases so they can bask in your brilliance. You and your Ham will be stars of the show."

"They'll be curious about *you*, Lady Violet. Rumors have begun about how you've discovered so many murderers."

Violet laughed as they walked up the steps to Mr. Morgan's well-lit house. "I think you mean they've discovered and targeted me. The only reason anyone talks about it at all is that I went shopping in London when I had my cracked ribs and broken collarbone. If I hadn't lost my wardrobe, I wouldn't have been caught out to start the rumor mill spinning."

Mr. Morgan's butler opened the door as they approached up the steps.

"Oh, lovely," Jack said unhappily as they passed the parlor. "They're gathering in here."

Violet sympathized, then excused herself to go upstairs and freshen her makeup and hair, straighten her jewelry, and leave her wrap before returning to the party. When she exited her room, Jack was waiting.

"I didn't want to face them without you."

"You're avoiding another conversation with Miss Allen on your arm," Violet said, but she was pleased. "What's her intent, I wonder, to claim you like that? Perhaps she wishes to step back into her role as your beloved."

He grinned in reply, and she knew she'd gotten it right. "I need your protection, darling. Save me."

"Stop it with your nonsense." She winked at him and then buffed her nails on her shoulder. "I suppose I can sharpen my knives and prepare to defend your honor."

"Shall I give you a favor to carry into battle?"

They'd made it to the parlor, and Violet's laugh caused several heads to turn. Jack nodded in greeting to a few of them, and Mr. Morgan led his selected guests into dinner.

As they walked into the dining room, Violet heard one of the men saying, "I understand he's been quite a bit of trouble lately. They found him snooping through Professor Snag's office, and Snag kicked the boy out of his seminar."

"He's an ambitious lad who needs a keeper. That father of his does nothing but throw money at the problems the boy causes, and his sister is nearly as nosey as he is. Wouldn't mind him throwing money my way to put up with the boy. Suspect that's why Morgan added him to his lads despite all the ill feelings. Emily's father probably owns a good percentage of that Piccadilly Press if I have my guess."

Violet's brows lifted, but the gentlemen stopped speaking when they realized that Violet and Jack could hear them. Jack's face was a study in evenness and Violet had no idea what he was thinking from those comments. Did he care about what they were saying? He more than anyone here would have a good idea of the reality of that situation.

In the awkward opening, Jack introduced the men to Violet, and she saw their glances move from herself to someone behind her.

Violet didn't need to guess. The lilting voice that carried into the room was all the answer Vi needed. Miss Allen, indeed. Violet pasted a polite smile on her face as though she were entirely unbothered by the woman's presence.

They didn't linger over the late dinner, as the reception would be a late one as well. It was too hot for a feast, so Mr. Morgan had wisely offered cool soup, cold hams, bread and cheese. Perhaps not a typical dinner, but the right one for the weather. The men didn't stay for their smoke and port, and they moved as a group into the reception room where the first of the reception guests were arriving.

One of the earliest was Jeremiah Allen, who walked into the room with a bruise on his cheek and a flourish in his gestures. He nearly strutted as he took in the room, despite the new addition of the bruise. Violet lifted a brow just enough that Jack followed her gaze. They both glanced towards Emily Allen, who shot her brother a telling look before turning her back on him.

She wasn't the only one, either. Several of the other invited students were the lads interested in the science of investigation, and they seemed—as a group—to dislike Mr. Allen. Why? Surely Mr. Allen wasn't the first lad to brag about his connections in a place such as Oxford? On the whole, they were probably the most well-connected students in the world.

Violet watched the lads, pretending to listen to Jack and the men converse. One of the boys was a ginger lad with freckles and ears so red, they were purple. She expected smoke to come from the young man's ears as he watched Mr. Allen speaking to another of the students.

What had Mr. Allen done to infuriate this ginger fellow so? Violet wanted nothing more than to go talk to the young man. She did have an absurd love of the inanities of the human race. She glanced at Jack, who had started discussing a case with one of the police officers who'd arrived. They were discussing evidence and suspects that Violet had no knowledge of, nor did she care to know more. She squeezed his arm and excused herself before he could stop her.

Violet crossed to the bar, got herself a G&T, and then deliberately wandered in a way that made it seem as though she'd stumbled across the lad. She knocked herself into him, spilling a little of her drink on him, so she could apologize profusely.

"Oh, I *am* sorry!"

He looked up at her with wide, distressed, dark brown eyes. She felt a flash of remorse that was even greater.

"I am sorry," she repeated, this time far more fervently. "I really should have been watching where I was going. Do forgive me."

"Of course," he said. The distress in his gaze didn't ease, and Violet noted that the direction of his gaze was fixed on one of the pictures of the young woman that had caught Violet's attention previously.

"She is lovely, isn't she?" Violet's tone was careful.

"She was," the young man said. "She was..." He trailed off, turning his gaze.

"Was?" Violet's voice was low and tentative.

"Was." His jaw clenched, and Violet could see the muscle in his jaw move. "She...died."

"Oh, I am sorry," Violet said. "I am so very sorry." She set down her drink. "I do seem to be flubbing this up horribly, don't I?" She held out her hand. "Violet Carlyle."

The man blinked, startled by her forwardness. "Nathan Tanner."

"Are you one of Mr. Morgan's students?"

"I was," he snapped. He cleared his throat, looking at her in a bit of horror. "I'm Professor Snag's aide right now. I, well...I left Professor Morgan. I couldn't face it."

"Because of the young woman?"

"Rachael Morgan. Professor Morgan's niece. She died at the start of the year."

"I'm so sorry," Violet said again. She had no doubt that this young man was grieving the loss of the girl. He must have loved her. Was it reciprocated? Or was he an admirer from a distance? Violet cared very much about knowing.

"Professor Snag wasn't able to make the lecture," Mr. Tanner said distractedly. "He asked me to attend in his stead to take notes. I suppose I am free to leave now." He nodded at Violet in farewell. "Miss Carlyle."

"Mr. Tanner," she replied, watching his gaze fix on the picture again before he stumbled from the room. She noticed a bulge in his pocket and a small space on the mantel that had obviously not been empty earlier.

She wasn't sure what was there before, but she'd lay down a good amount of money on it being a small picture of the late and lovely Rachael Morgan.

Violet returned to the bar to refresh her cocktail, leaving Jack to his group of friends, and made her way to a chair on the side of the room. She was curious to see the rest of the young men interact with the professors, and she wanted to see the way the young Mr. Allen interacted with them all.

Vi had no intention of succumbing to the blackmail of Miss

Emily Allen. If Violet did, she would be an endless and easy target for the vile woman. Violet had little doubt that a woman who would blackmail once would do so again.

Mr. Allen's gaze had followed Nathan Tanner as he left, as did several of the other university lads. What did they know? Their looks certainly seemed intent. Violet admitted she'd become entranced by the drama of these university lads. She'd like to discover more about their personal traumas and possibly add them to her next book.

CHAPTER SIX

*V*iolet grinned as Mr. Barnes sat down with her. "Well, my dear, I fear our evening has descended into one of your pulp novels. Former, betraying lovers appear out of nowhere. Fisticuffs before the party if young Mr. Allen's face is to be believed. Swaggering and rather a lot of posturing." Mr. Barnes smiled winningly at her. "May I jump to first names with you, my dear? I have felt quite encumbered making it clear that you were my friend when I referred to you as Lady Violet."

Violet winked at him. "Alike, my dear friend, alike, alike." She had noted the careful use of the word 'betraying' with a surge of gratitude. Jack was too honorable to tell tales on Miss Allen. She appreciated that Hamilton was not.

"Was the evening all you wished?"

"Posturing, Violet. These evenings are more about skipping about on our laurels than sharing knowledge. That's what the journal articles are for."

Violet laughed as Mr. Morgan took another seat near Hamilton and Violet. Before he could speak, the room cleared, giving them a clear view of an argument between the young men. Mr. Barnes and Violet stared as one of the two university lads shoved Mr. Allen. His sister was watching impassively from the sidelines.

Jack stepped in before the young man could respond, and a moment later, he was escorting all of them from the reception room.

"My goodness," Mr. Morgan sputtered. "I will be having words with those lads. Apologies, Lady Violet, Ham."

Hamilton laughed. "I enjoy the ridiculous, my friend. This seems to be bringing the evening to a swift close rather than a slow, stuttering end. You'd best see them out before they stampede. Miss Allen left with quite a scowl, did you see? I suspect she didn't get what she wanted for her article."

Mr. Morgan lifted one of those domineering eyebrows and said, "Dealing with Emily calls for a drink."

He rose, leaving the two of them to their shadowy corner, while the remaining guests seemed to decide as one to leave. When he returned, his butler followed with a tray of cocktails.

"My man made the drinks according to the directions your brother sent along with those quite welcome bottles of rum, Lady Violet. Come Ham, try this drink. It's called an El Presidente. I've saved it for the four of us when we're putting up our feet after the evening."

Violet set aside her half-finished G&T and took up the fresh cocktail glass. She'd only been holding the G&T to prevent someone from handing her a new drink. The El Presidente did sound lovely, however. With grenadine, white rum, black vermouth and—most welcome of all—ice chips, she took a sip and sighed at the coolness of it. With the windows opened and the press of bodies gone, the room was finally starting to cool.

"That's quite the thing, isn't it," Mr. Morgan said. "Where did your brother come up with the recipe?"

"He became quite good friends with a barman when we were in Cuba."

"That's right, Jack went to Cuba as well, didn't he?"

Violet nodded. Her head tilted as she examined the two men. "Why were the students fighting like that?"

Mr. Morgan laughed heartily as he shrugged, which told Violet he both knew and had no intention of telling her.

Hamilton, on the other hand, said, "Young Allen is a bit of a know-it-all upstart who is actually clever. It's quite irritating, I think, for all of us. He's been writing to me for months now about his ideas. At first..." Hamilton smiled awkwardly.

Violet could imagine. At first it had been flattering, maybe even a mentoring moment. Violet knew the power of it. She had it with her sister, Isolde, as well as young Ginny, and even Anna Mathers. Both of those girls looked up to Violet. It made her feel as though she had to be all the more careful. She couldn't mess up, because in making mistakes, she might lead the girls down the wrong path, ruining their lives with the simple miscalculations of her own.

"Why Cuba?" Mr. Morgan asked, changing the subject back.

Violet grinned merrily. "It was an article my brother read about rum cocktails. I suppose we're just—"

"Delightfully frivolous," Hamilton finished for her as Jack returned.

His evening jacket was askew, and he straightened it before taking the seat next to Violet and accepting a cocktail. "El Presidente? I've had the memory of its flavor for a few weeks now. I should have had Victor make me one."

"He's moved through quite a bit of the rum," Violet told him.

"I think he's about to send poor Hargreaves all the way to Cuba to retrieve more."

"You bright young things—" Mr. Morgan bit off the term and shook his head. "Going to Cuba for cocktails."

Jack crossed his leg over his knee. "They had sun and sand too, Daniel. Cuba's quite a lovely country, and I'd recommend a trip given the chance."

"But cocktails, Jack, by Jove, man. At least come up with another reason to visit a place."

Jack shook his head and clinked his drink with Violet. "Don't be confused, my friend. Many of these bright young things are as clever as Violet and her brother."

"The cocktail man? Not intending to be offensive, Lady Violet. Not at all…"

Violet laughed and lifted her cocktail to Mr. Morgan. "I am not offended, Mr. Morgan. We are frivolous. Lazy, even."

"You aren't lazy, Vi."

"We can be," Violet told Jack. "I was quite lazy in Cuba."

"You wrote a novel in Cuba, sharpened your Spanish, made friends with several young urchins and assisted their mother with that issue."

"I also drank too much rum and ate my weight in torticas de Morón and ropa vieja. Don't make up attributes for me, Jack. We can't pretend that I'm not a spoiled toff who gets drunk more often than I should and attends far too many middle-of-the-night treasure hunts or fancy dress parties. Tell me what the fisticuffs were about. These fine fellows are protecting my delicate sensibilities."

Jack lifted a brow at Violet. "Fine. Violet is frivolous and lazy. She has little, if anything, to recommend her. The boys…who knows? Young Allen was pretty upset and kept trying to get me to take a few minutes to listen to him, but he was also so angry he was incomprehensible."

Violet's mouth twisted. "The poor kid. Everything was so serious back in our schooldays."

"Did you go to university?" Mr. Morgan asked, sounding surprised.

Violet nodded and took another sip of her cocktail.

"She's leaving out the first she took." Jack sounded as if he were bragging about her, and Violet shot him a surprised look.

"It's of little import." Violet set her cocktail aside. She was looking forward to a morning on the water with Jack and their picnic and didn't want to do it with a headache. "And now I believe I will leave you to your cocktails and cases."

She left the gentlemen to make her way to her room.

There had been smoking through the evening along with the press of bodies, and she wanted to remove the scent, and the sweat, from her skin. She missed having her maid Beatrice with her as she filled her bath and dug out her nightgown, bath items, and kimono. She had to laugh at herself at the thought and quickly scrubbed away the scents of the evening, rubbing lavender oil into her skin. She got out of the bath, wiped away the cold cream on her face and removed the last remnants of her makeup before preparing her hair for the next day and laying out her clothes.

She folded the coverlet and blankets to the end of the bed and crawled under only the sheet. As she placed her eye mask over her face, she recalled the look on her brother's face as he asked what she and Jack would be doing on their trip. Why had he asked? What had Victor been up to? Her eyes would have narrowed if she'd had them opened. Instead, she turned onto her side.

The day flashed through her mind. The lovely Miss Allen,

who—Violet now realized—regretted the loss of Jack. The young Mr. Allen, who had asked for help in the worst possible way. If only he'd been less abrasive.

Mr. Morgan, who had been both kind and a bit condescending. The lovely Hamilton Barnes, who had taken her side. Violet took in a long breath, blanked her mind and let sleep claim her.

CHAPTER SEVEN

*T*he day dawned bright and beautiful and *hot*. Violet dressed accordingly with a long, loose skirt, a loose sailor's style blouse, and a wide-brimmed hat to protect her complexion from the sun. She didn't bother with powder, but she did apply a light layer of pink lipstick, a little rouge on her cheeks, and a ring on her right hand, so she could fiddle with it. She slipped a couple of simple bangles on her wrist for the same reason.

After she dressed, she arranged her bedroom, sorting it out. She couldn't abide messes, and it was a quick few minutes to return her manuscript to her satchel, put her dress from the previous evening into her suitcase, and lock up the jewelry she wasn't wearing. She and Jack would return for their bags before they left Oxford to take the last train back to London.

Violet glanced around the bedroom and started. Her copy of *The Black Mask* magazine had fallen from the bedside table to the floor under the bed. She'd have been distressed if she hadn't been able to finish the detective story she was halfway through. She placed that in her satchel as well. She scanned the room a final time, then gathered her handbag with her lipstick, powder, house key, and money.

Jack was waiting with a basket when Violet joined him. They ate a quick breakfast alone, for Mr. Morgan was already off to his office at the university and Hamilton had either not left his room or had already left the house. Violet rather thought it was the latter.

Jack had arranged a boat for them, and they made their way to the river through the town with Jack carrying the basket and Violet walking at his side.

"It's so lovely here."

Jack nodded silently, and she wondered once more what, if anything, bothered him. Was he thinking of Miss Allen? She had been upset the evening before when she'd left, but Violet had stuck to the sidelines, watching the university people interact. When Miss Allen had left in a huff, Violet hadn't been part of the conversation, and she hadn't had a chance to ask Jack more about it.

She decided to shake off her worries. Surely some fresh air and the coolness of the water would cheer him and return Jack to his normal self.

"I've been thinking about making another young ingénue for our next books," Violet told him, trying to draw him out of his thoughts. "Maybe two or three about the same girl? Victor wants to write about a young lad who gets shanghaied. I think we might actually fight about our story. Though, I do confess I am becoming more and more intrigued by a detective story. I *do* love reading them."

Jack laughed at that and Violet felt as though things were right again. "You two don't fight."

"We do! Don't pretend like you don't know how fierce we are.

You were a witness last time. What did Lila call it? The titans rumbling?"

Jack grinned but refused to agree with Violet. "Lila is almost as dramatic as Denny is lazy. Are they still dealing with that sister of hers?"

"Martha? Intrepid and slightly villainess. Ooh, that is an idea. We could turn Martha into a villain and then write her as a foil for our heroine. I shall have to bring it up to Victor. I believe he should like to torture young Martha on the page."

Jack grunted, seemingly not listening again even though he replied readily enough. "He should be grateful to Lila's bedamned sister. Without her, you'd not have asked Kate to rescue Victor, and he wouldn't have tripped so easily into love."

Violet grinned at that. She was swinging her free hand as they walked, enjoying the cooler morning air, even if Jack insisted on being distracted. As they approached the boathouse, she found that Jack had arranged for things to be fully ready. He stepped into a waiting boat, lifted her down, and they were on the water a moment later. The boy who had been hired to get the boat and make it ready was paid, and they were on their way.

The breeze picked up and Violet sighed into it.

"What a perfect day," she told him. "If we have so many more hot days, I may be unable to continue living. Has Hades found its way to earth?"

Jack only nodded. Violet fought to keep a frown off of her face as she watched Jack row the boat. She decided she must let the worry go and enjoy the breeze off the water and the refreshing feel of being on the river.

Jack rowed the boat while Violet relaxed, letting her fingers trail in the water while they made their way past the few others on the river. It was a weekday, so it wasn't as crowded as a Saturday or Sunday would have been even though it was also the holidays, and there were few students who were rowing. Violet appreciated the solitude of the river in general.

"Look at them," Violet said, nodding towards an older couple. They were in a similar position as Jack and Violet, with the woman reading to the man while he rowed on the water. They were decades older, but Violet felt as though she was looking into the future, if she were very lucky.

"Violet..."

Vi looked up. Jack...by Jove! Was he blushing? His face was actually flushed. His ears were red. Was he sick? Surely the rowing hadn't been too much.

"Violet..."

"Jack?"

"I..." He pulled his collar away from his neck and cleared his throat. "I...I've been looking for the way to...put this..."

She blinked rapidly, sitting upright. "Are you all right?"

"It doesn't come naturally to me."

"Rowing?"

"Words. Ah...emotions. I was trying for romantic like Lila ordered, but I fear I've failed. And now, here we are, and I don't think I can return without telling you..."

Violet reached out and took Jack's hand. "It's all right, Jack. Is there anything wrong?"

"Nothing is wrong, darling. I only...I wanted to ask you..."

Violet suddenly understood. Her mouth dropped open for a moment and then she took tighter hold of his hand, suspecting her own cheeks were flushed and her own ears brilliantly red. Her heart was racing, and she wasn't sure she'd have been able to stop the trembling of her hands if she hadn't been holding onto his hand quite so hard.

"Marry me? Will you marry me?" He simply stopped talking

and stared at her, but he raised his hand to cup her cheek. "Don't say no."

He rubbed his thumb along her chin as she started to answer, leaning forward until their foreheads were pressed together. She'd have told him yes immediately, but her heart had seized and her voice was stolen. She could feel the tears in her eyes as she tried to find the breath to tell him yes.

"I—"

A scream rent the air and they jerked apart, turning to face the older couple. The woman was grasping her chest and the man was leaning over the side of the boat.

"Help! By God, someone help us!"

Violet gasped, twisting to see. She could see the older man getting out of his boat. He was struggling with an object in the reeds while his wife looked conflicted by whether she should be crying or screaming and was alternating between her options.

Jack swung the boat towards them as quickly as possible, and they both rowed to get to the other couple. Violet reached out and took the woman's hand as they pulled their two small rowboats together. She followed the woman's horrified gaze to the water where her husband was standing in the shadows. A moment later, Jack cursed and stepped out.

He was, perhaps, merely better prepared for what they had found. Violet had expected, well, she hadn't been sure what to expect. Having Jack thrust the oars into her hands as her mind tried to make sense of what she was seeing wasn't it.

She noted the hand first. Her mind hadn't been able to make it anything other than a man's hand. The fingers curled towards the palm, the skin swollen, water-logged and wrong, but still a hand.

She squeezed tightly on the hand of the older woman, the two of them transfixed on the sight of the men they loved working with the body. The man's dark jacket was floating, his riotous hair tangled with the reed.

"We just...stumbled across him," the woman said.

Neither Violet nor Jack answered. Carefully, Jack turned the body over with the help of the woman's husband.

All of them gasped at the sight. Violet turned aside, choking back her emotions and wishing—wishing so hard—that the face was a stranger's. After seeking help and being sent away, Jeremiah Allen was dead.

CHAPTER EIGHT

"*V*i, I need Ham," Jack said. He paused long enough to meet her gaze, regret in those penetrating eyes as he added, "and the local boys."

"Of course." She glanced at the woman. "You should come with me."

Her husband looked up at his wife, taking in her trembling lips, her shaking hands, and the tears on her face. "Go with her, Margaret. The young woman will see you home after she gets the bobbies."

Violet inclined her head, and the woman carefully shifted from her rowboat to Violet's. Jack approached Violet, leaning in to whisper to her, so only she could hear.

"Vi, there's signs of a struggle on the body. The bruise has compatriots now. His eye is swollen. There's a wound on the back of his head as though he'd been hit with a heavy object and scratches on his hands. I doubt very much this was an accident. Tell Ham."

Jack pulled back, his gaze weighted. Violet nodded silently.

The other couple had been watching Jack whisper to Violet, but she was fairly sure that they hadn't heard.

"I'll have Ham here quickly," she promised. Jack gave them a mighty shove to get the boat moving, and she used the momentum to propel them forward.

"That poor boy. That poor boy," Margaret said over and over again. She was sniffling into a massive handkerchief that Violet suspected was her husband's.

Violet rowed for all she was worth, chased by the phantasm of his poor older sister trying to get help for her brother. Guilt assailed her as she rowed. If she hadn't been so angry, she'd have talked to Jack on Miss Allen's behalf despite their history. Violet would have done most of it differently if Miss Allen hadn't threatened her. Did Miss Allen's behavior somehow absolve Violet?

No. It didn't feel like it at all.

Violet was working against the current on the way back and would have happily let Jack do the rowing if the day had gone as it should.

Violet nearly dropped an oar when she remembered what came before the body. Jack had proposed.

Selfish though it might be, Violet felt a rush of fury that her moment had been stolen from her. She hadn't even gotten to tell him yes. She hadn't been able to throw herself at him or even let her tears out.

A tear slipped down her face at the conflict of emotions, frustration for the lost moment, shock at what had happened to Mr. Allen, horror that they might have been able to stop it if they hadn't avoided him. And the guilt for feeling so frustrated and angry for what should have been one of the happiest days of her life being ruined by yet another body.

Why, by the heavens, *why* did people do these things to each other? What could a boy, who had been so young, have possibly done to incite someone to murder? He had been irritating. That had been evident. But surely you just threw him in the river and then laughed at the soaked young man. You didn't murder him.

Violet pulled the boat up to the dock Margaret indicated and they hurried for the police station. Violet burst through the door and declared, "There's a body in the river."

The policeman slowly stood up, blinking in shock.

"Someone drowned?"

Violet glanced at Margaret and they both shook their heads.

"My dear," the policeman said, "don't imagine the worst."

"I was with my friend, Jack Wakefield. Perhaps you've heard of him? He's an investigator, and he stated that it was a murder."

"Wakefield?" The policeman looked blankly at Violet. He didn't seem to know the name. A part of Violet smirked, and the rest of her was shrieking in irritation.

"Jack Wakefield. He works for Scotland Yard. Please—"

Margaret cut in with a sensibleness that only someone who had so much experience could add. "It doesn't really matter, man. Go find the body, talk to her friend yourself. Either way, there's a dead boy in the river."

Margaret explained where to find them and Violet waited only long enough to ensure Margaret had the policeman in hand before she excused herself to get Mr. Barnes. She rushed towards the university. Mr. Barnes had intended to spend the morning talking with Mr. Morgan about his research.

Violet debated. Should she run to the house and the servants who knew where Mr. Barnes would be? Or should she rush to the university and try to hunt up the office of Mr. Morgan? She made a decision and ran for the house. She slammed into the door, out of breath and trying to catch it while she rang the bell repeatedly.

The butler swung the door open and Violet didn't give him a chance to say anything. "Mr. Barnes? Is he in?"

The butler shook his head.

"Send someone for him at once. No...I...I'll...write a note. I need a paper and pen."

The butler heard the urgency in Violet's voice and told her to follow him.

"The master said they'd be back soon, my lady."

Violet nodded, still struggling to catch her breath. She held one hand to her side and told herself she really should exercise more. Violet cleared her throat, trying to find enough air to speak. "There's been a terrible accident at the river. Jack needs Mr. Barnes right away."

The butler's gaze widened, but he kept that smooth, professional expression that seemed to be inherent to butlers everywhere. Violet began to write a note when there was noise at the front door. "I'll get Mr. Barnes if that's him," the butler said.

Violet continued writing in case it wasn't him. She didn't have it in her to make another race across Oxford. She wasn't terribly out of shape, but she had been in full sprint. She sniffed back emotions as she penned what had occurred and what Jack had said. Then the door of the office opened and Mr. Barnes entered.

"I understand you need me, Lady Violet?"

"Mr. Barnes, thank goodness!"

"Are you all right? I confess—"

She shook her head to cut him off and help up a hand. "Jeremiah Allen is dead. Jack says it's murder. The body was in the shallows on the river. I sent the local police, but Jack said to get you, too."

Mr. Barnes moved with speed at her words, demanding what information she could give, and then he was gone. Violet sank into a nearby chair, staring at the wall and seeing the bloated face of Mr. Allen once again. She shuddered at the memory, wishing she could scour her mind.

"Lady Violet?" The butler's smooth, even voice cut into the terrible memory, and she looked up with gratitude. "I thought tea? Or lemonade? I've brought both."

Violet stared at him for too long, blinking stupidly until she finally pushed herself to her feet. "In my room, I think."

The butler nodded and followed her up the stairs with the tray. He placed it on the vanity table and asked, "May I get you anything else?"

Violet considered. What she wanted was Jack, but she knew she wouldn't be getting him while he was dealing with atrocity.

"My brother. Mr. Victor Carlyle." Violet added the telephone number and begged the butler to send for him. She was assured that her brother would be contacted, and Violet returned to the chair in front of the vanity, pouring herself both a cup of tea and a glass of lemonade. She stared at it stupidly until she forced herself to drink it, and then she crossed to her packed satchel, removing her journal and her favorite pen.

She wrote out what she'd observed regarding Mr. Allen for the last few days. She wondered what he'd done to engender so much hatred towards him. Surely he couldn't be an innocent victim of circumstance, not after the tensions had been running high. Not after his sister had asked for help on his behalf.

Violet flinched at the thought of Emily Allen. She rose to pace as she thought about Miss Allen. She knew about being a sister. She was a twin sister, a younger sister, and an older sister. Violet supposed that given their ages, Miss Allen losing Jeremiah was akin to Violet losing Isolde. She ached at the idea. She'd be devastated to lose her younger sister.

When would Jack tell Miss Allen that Jeremiah was dead? Violet had no doubt it would be Jack, who didn't know that Miss Allen had tried to blackmail Violet into getting help for her brother. Would he be furious with Vi if he found out? She'd intended to tell him on the way back from the river. She hadn't wanted their day ruined by Miss Allen's intentions.

Violet had already decided that, as for herself, she would not have pretended to bargain with Miss Allen. Sooner or later, someone would out the twins. Violet was only grateful it had been her who had slipped instead of one of their friends. Too many knew that Violet and Victor were V.V. Twinnings. It was a secret that was bound to be revealed.

She paced the room, fiddling with the ring she'd placed on her finger earlier that day. Back and forth, back and forth she went, not able to grasp the details. She knew she'd had a shock. It wasn't that she was helpless against what had happened so much as she needed some time to gather her thoughts, to process through all the things assailing her. She needed to clear and organize her mind. She'd gone through this far too often.

Often she could do that through writing, but Violet didn't think that at the moment she'd be able to gather her thoughts with a pen yet. Instead she removed her shoes and started to practice the Jiu-Jitsu forms that she'd been learning.

Victor had found both Violet and Kate a teacher. He'd even found a female one. Violet moved through the forms until her body was covered in sweat and her muscles were shaking. When she finished, she hadn't managed to put her thoughts in order, but she was less stunned. Violet sighed and walked to the bath off of her bedroom. If nothing else, she'd have a cool bath and examine her dress options for the evening. She'd intended on traveling for their return in the clothes she'd been wearing and hadn't packed additional options.

Violet dug through her clothes, wrapped up in her kimono with her hair in a towel. She dressed herself in the clothes she'd worn that first day on the train. They were a little worse for the wear, but they were the best option she had. She sighed as she dressed, then rang the bell for the butler.

He arrived after a few minutes. It was late in the evening, and no one had returned. She'd have been upset if she didn't know they were all occupied by what was truly important.

"Were you able to reach my brother?"

"Yes, my lady. He said he'll be on his way. He had me find a hotel for him, which I have done."

Violet realized she should join her brother and sighed as she gave instructions to ensure a suite of rooms with a sitting room and a bedroom for each of them, if it was possible.

The butler left, stating that the servants would have dinner for Violet soon. Should she change back into her evening gown? But no. She expected she'd be dining alone and that Jack would get back to her as soon as he could.

She settled into the chair at the desk and found herself staring. Her mouth twisted as the butler returned to say they'd been able to find a suite of rooms at a nearby hotel. Violet nodded. "Did you know Jeremiah Allen?" she asked him before he could leave.

He hesitated. "He was around quite a bit with the other university lads up until Miss Rachael died. Mr. Morgan stopped inviting the lads over after her death. I haven't seen much of them since those sad days."

"Was he well liked?"

The butler considered before speaking. "He was awkward, my lady. The older lads had worked hard for their positions, and he was very young to be included."

"What about Miss Rachael?" She wasn't quite sure what made her ask, but the perfect evenness of the butler's expressions were finally challenged.

"Miss Rachael was beloved by all of us, my lady. She was good and kind and friendly, and those lads—like everyone who knew her—loved her."

It was apparent that Violet had bothered the butler, so she said, "Thank you. I suppose I'm trying to make sense of it. It's not fair, losing Miss Rachael or this boy, Mr. Allen. It doesn't seem to matter how many times we lose someone. It strikes a blow every time, even though I didn't know either of them. I never had the pleasure to even meet Miss Rachael, but I shall always regret that now."

It was the right thing to say, and it was the honest truth for Violet. Mr. Morgan's butler accepted her comments and seemed to forgive her for too overtly meddling into the life of his beloved mistress.

"It's hard for all of us, my lady. She was sunshine in this house. You're the first young woman we've had among us since she died. She...this was her room. Simply having someone in it again is bittersweet, I suppose."

Violet would have reached out and squeezed his hand, but she was sure that her touch would be unwelcome, so she let him press fresh tea on her despite the nearness of the dinner she'd be eating alone. A daily maid brought up the next tea tray, and Violet took it with gratitude even though she didn't want it. She made herself a cup of tea as she looked around the room with new eyes.

Miss Rachael Morgan's sanctuary was a lovely room. Violet had noted it when she'd been placed into it, but she hadn't realized that there was personality to the room. The pretty little vanity table had been bought for someone. The linens and coverlet had been chosen for her specifically. The room was sweet and friendly and welcoming, as Violet understood Miss Rachael had been.

Violet examined the desk again, opening the drawers, but there was nothing to be seen. The vanity drawers had been empty when Violet had unpacked her belongings. The bureau of drawers had been empty as well, though Violet had only glanced over them and then placed her case in the armoire.

Was it idle wishing that made Violet want to search the room and—for that matter—Mr. Morgan's library and office? Wishing that Violet could somehow uncover a clue in the house she'd been left in that would bring matters to a close? Or was it more that she wanted to be useful? There was little reason to believe that Mr. Morgan or his niece had anything to do with Jeremiah's death. And yet... she did need to do something with her time.

The dinner gong rang for the lone Violet, who ate by herself and returned to the bedroom. She had no expectation of finding anything, and yet she decided she might as well put on the meddling hat of one of her ingénues and pass her evening by searching Miss Morgan's bedroom.

CHAPTER NINE

*V*iolet expected to find nothing searching a dead girl's room. The truth was she wanted to distract herself from what she'd seen. Every other time she'd faced this sort of horror, she'd had family and friends. The first time— when her sister Isolde's soon-to-be-jilted fiancé was killed, Violet's twin had gotten her drunk. He'd given her whiskey and tea until she was sleeping and weeping, transferring between the two states without even realizing what was happening around her.

Being in a stranger's home alone, with the sight of poor Mr. Allen's dead body in her head, was extremely unwelcome for a woman who nearly always had people around her. She was realizing that she was, perhaps, more dependent on her brother than she'd prefer to admit. Violet opened the window seat and stared into it, wishing for her brother.

"You are a wet blanket, Vi," she told herself. She should have curled up with her detective magazine. "Perhaps not a wet blanket. You are a delicate flower. Those militant female types who have been working for the vote would be disgusted with you, my dear."

The evening had lengthened into the dark hours when she heard the front door open. Her joy at realizing Jack had returned and she was no longer alone with the servants electrified her, and she forced herself to stay on her knees near the window seat until she'd gathered control of herself.

It took a few minutes for footsteps on the stairs, and Violet was ready by that point. She opened her door to see Jack with bags under his eyes and a tight expression. Hamilton was behind Jack, and Violet's gaze flicked from one to the other. They both looked exhausted and perhaps sick by what they'd experienced that day.

"Did you eat?" she asked.

Hamilton shook his head. "Daniel is having his servants bring up a tray for the each of us."

Violet couldn't stop from asking, "It was murder?" Jack nodded once while Hamilton hesitated.

Jack cursed and muttered to his friend, "She's a magnet for murders, and she's too clever for us to pull the wool over her eyes."

"It's hardly her fault that you took her on the water where they dumped the body," Hamilton said. It was clear by his statement that Jack had discussed his intentions with Hamilton. Had they discussed how the proposal had been interrupted at just the wrong moment?

Violet wasn't sure how to answer him now. She could see murder at the forefront of his mind rather than love. She was selfish enough to admit that when she finally told him that she loved him and that there was nothing she wanted more than to be his, she wanted to be the only thing on his mind.

"True," Jack said. He tangled his fingers with Violet's,

squeezing them lightly. Perhaps they were having a moment where they agreed to wait on the proposal? Or was he wishing she'd answer him now? She wasn't going to satisfy that desire if he did. Murders had intruded on too much of their lives as it was. She wasn't going to allow one to ruin this momentous part of their lives, even if it meant they had to wait.

Jack finally spoke again, telling Hamilton, "She's a meddler. I suppose I should get used to her being in trouble. That last case didn't have anything to do with Violet and yet there she was...involved."

Violet gasped, trying for a merry sound and only partially succeeding. "I am innocent! Alas. Woe. Cruel, cruel fate." She sobered before asking Hamilton, "Were you asked to assist on this case?"

"We were," Hamilton said. "I think we both feel..."

"Guilty," Jack finished. "That boy had been trying to get both of our attention, and we ignored him, and now he's dead."

"It's not your fault," Violet told them, as though she didn't feel as guilty.

"It's the killer's fault," Hamilton agreed, "but we're always going to wonder if there was something we could have done. It's simply the nature of it, Violet."

Jack didn't nod, but Violet was sure that he felt the same. She knew she did.

"I sent for Victor," Jack told Violet.

It wasn't as though Violet needed a man to look after her, but she knew that Jack was trying to protect her. And probably keep her out of his case. She admitted, "As did I. I assumed you'd be asked to assist and didn't want you worrying over me."

"Thank you, Violet." There was an intense feeling behind that statement that warmed her.

There was a click, and she realized that Hamilton had stepped into his bedroom, leaving them alone. She opened her arms to Jack, and he took the hug she offered. It was a comforting thing. The press of their bodies against each other, the placing of her cheek on his chest, the sound of his heartbeat in her ear—they both needed it.

"Are you all right?"

He tensed in her arms. "I'm still thinking what-ifs."

"As am I," Violet told him. "Miss Allen tried to get me to convince you to help him. I intended to tell you after our time on the river, but..."

"It was too late," Jack said.

Violet nodded.

"I have to get up early, Vi. I can't prevent what happened to poor Jeremy any more than I can turn back time. If I could, I would. But I *will* find who did this, and they *will* pay."

Jack kissed her forehead and left her a moment later. She stared after him, watching the door to his bedroom close before she returned to her room and put on her nightgown. She didn't like to see the guilt on his face or the way his shoulders were bowing under the weight of this case. She didn't like to think that he'd always wonder what-if.

She knew he'd called for Victor to keep her safe. She was sure, in fact, that Jack assumed Victor would take Violet home in Jack's stead. He underestimated both of the twins, if he thought that was so, though that wouldn't be the first time.

There was her unfortunate capacity to be sucked into—or perhaps meddle—in Jack's investigations. Had she meddled in the past? To herself, Violet would admit that she had. She would again—this time. If there was something Violet could do to help alleviate the guilt pressing down on him, Violet would do it.

For him. For her. For their future. She knew he wouldn't want her to. She'd been in danger too often in the past because of her tendency to meddle. That was why she let her Jiu-Jitsu trainer, Mayako, beat her into a more dangerous version of herself.

Violet wasn't foolish, and she had fallen in love with a man who investigated murders—not for a living but simply because he was very, very good at it. Which was why, when he wanted to add firing a gun to her skills, she hadn't argued. She had known then she'd get drawn into another case in the future, and she had no intention of being unable to defend herself.

She hadn't expected the next time she meddled to be quite so soon, and a part of her had wished it would never come. It seemed she was doomed to disappointment.

CHAPTER TEN

The morning dawned bright and beautiful, and Violet woke to the sound of a knock on her bedroom door. She pushed back her eye mask and crossed the room, expecting to see Jack. It was, however, her maid, Beatrice.

"My lady? Are you all right? Mr. Victor said you'd want to be woken up and have the things I brought."

"I do want clothes! My goodness, I am never traveling without extra options again." Violet placed both hands on Beatrice's cheeks and squeezed. She winked as she let the girl into the room. While Violet took the case from Beatrice, the maid arranged the room and put Violet's things away.

"We arrived yesterday quite late," Beatrice told Violet. "Mr. Victor said you'd rather know we've arrived than have a lie-in."

"He was right," Violet said, dressing quickly. Her dress was another thin one that hung loosely on her body to provide the chance for a bit of air, even though the hot days were making that unlikely.

"You wish to move to the hotel with Mr. Victor?"

Both no and yes was the answer, but she had no desire to stay where she'd be left behind as the gentlemen went about their investigation. Jack was probably already gone and working, trying to find out the events leading to poor Jeremiah Allen's death.

Beatrice gathered the last of her things while Violet left her bedroom and went down the stairs to her brother. She almost threw herself at him but held back. She pretended a calmness that she was not feeling. He didn't buy it for a second and opened his arms to her. With the silent invitation, she did throw herself at him.

"You found his body on the water?" Victor's voice was low and familiar.

Violet nodded. Victor hesitated, waiting, and Violet realized suddenly that he'd *known* that Jack was going to propose. Of course Victor had. Knowing Jack, he'd asked for both Victor's blessing and her father's. In fact, knowing Jack, he'd probably asked for Victor's blessing first.

Violet punched her brother on his arm for hiding Jack's play from her.

"You...you...ah! You're supposed to be on my side."

Victor smirked and chucked her softly on the chin. "I *am* on your side, Violet. It's why I told Jack that a proposal on the water would be just the thing. I know you better and know you'd rather have him give his heart without the fanfare of romance that doesn't match the man you love."

Violet considered for a second. He was right. She hadn't needed Jack to write her a poem that was mostly plagiarized. She'd wanted his words, not someone else's. She thought back, bypassing the body in the water and made herself focus on what happened before. That nearly desperate, *Marry me? Will you marry me? Don't say no.* The final, that order, it was so Jack. Violet wasn't sure that there was any statement more assuring of his love than his demand that she not say no.

"So you're engaged then? Of course you didn't say no. I will now welcome him to the twindom and begin to torture him."

Violet shook her head, and Victor's jaw dropped. "You didn't say no. You couldn't have. My goodness, Vi—"

"I said nothing!" Violet shoved at her brother, breaking away, so she could pace. "That stupid boy was murdered and a woman started screaming the second I started to answer. I..."

Victor closed his mouth. His eyes glinted with humor, and Violet smacked him each time she passed him while she paced.

"Kate is back," Victor said. "I've left her at the hotel with Ginny."

"You brought them?"

"I'm not an idiot, Vi. You might have called for me, but you aren't leaving Oxford until this case is solved."

A slow smile passed over her face. "Jack thinks you'll bring me home."

"Oh, Jack," Victor sighed, then followed it with an evil chuckle. "Poor Jack. In love and so very blind."

Violet's echoing evil chuckle escaped. "I needed clothes and someone to meddle with me."

"I knew what you wanted. You sent a blind plea for help. Jack sent me a wire to come and get you. He's naïve yet."

Violet grinned as Beatrice stuck her head into the room. "I've got your things, Lady Violet. Mr. Giles and I will take them to the hotel if you didn't need anything else."

Violet shook her head and turned back to her brother.

"There is much you need to know, but let's start with the most important." Violet told him of meeting Miss Allen.

"What now?" Victor said at the end of Violet's tale.

"A former fiancé," Vi reiterated, focusing on the part that mattered the most.

"And she figured out we were V. V. Twinnings?" Victor shook his head. "Of course she did. You must have been dumbfounded when you met her."

"Pole-axed. Mouth hanging open, catching flies. Floundering for purchase. All of it."

"Bloody hell," Victor muttered. "I forget sometimes how well you've trained me to think the way women think. Jack is lucky I've correspondingly trained you to think more like a man, or he'd have been facing a jealous ninny who was certain he'd been lying the whole time."

Violet passed her brother in her pacing, smacking him again. "Not all women are jealous ninnies, you fool. Do you think that Kate would immediately leap to assuming you've been lying and that you never loved her?"

"No," Victor muttered, "but that's why I love her."

"No one group of people is true to their stereotypes, my love. Don't be an idiot."

Victor shot Violet a quelling look, but she ignored him as she returned to pacing. She told him what she'd witnessed with Jeremiah Allen, and the way that Miss Allen had attempted to black-mail Violet—and Victor for that matter.

"By Jove, Violet! Lady Eleanor is going to be a devil when she discovers the books."

Violet winced and nodded.

He sighed, his gaze flicking over her face before he said, "I shall have to get Kate to elope with me before her mother discovers what we've been up to. Mrs. Lancaster seems to expect better from us since we financed that orphanage. At least dear Stepmother assumes we're up to something she'd despise."

"True enough," Violet said. She did her best to explain how

Jeremiah Allen was Emily Allen's brother and how he had seemingly purchased his way into being one of Mr. Morgan's research lads. The way the research assistants clearly had some discontent between them.

"There's a dead niece?" Victor asked. "Who the lads all liked?"

"According to the butler," Violet admitted. "Who is clearly still mourning her."

"She'd only matter if we were writing a book. She's probably only a poor girl who got quite ill and didn't recover."

Violet's mouth twisted. She supposed she was using the links she'd make in a book on this case. Why were people murdered? Money, love, to hide another crime, betrayal, obsession, revenge. Most often, at least in Violet's experience, it had been for love. Twisted love, coming from a sick person who didn't understand what it meant to truly love.

"If he were a woman, I would say we should look towards who supposedly loved her. As a young man? Maybe it was a monetary crime? Or an act of like...anger gone wrong? Fisticuffs and an accident?"

Victor shook his head. "People aren't so easy to kill, Violet. It's not like you give someone a solid knock and they fall down dead. You, of all people, know that."

"You got hurt in that last case too, Victor," she snapped.

"So, I should know it as well, then. Perhaps you accidentally kill someone with a gun that you didn't mean to shoot. Or perhaps you accidentally kill someone in an auto accident or stumbling and knocking them down from a high place. It isn't what happened here, Violet."

She nodded, continuing to pace. "I need to tell Jack where we're staying. I'd like to see where it is."

Violet rang the bell and asked the butler for paper and a pen. She wrote Jack a letter explaining where she was and another note to Hamilton requesting him to keep a close eye on Jack. It didn't matter to her that they were both strong men and professionals. Jack had become vital to her happiness.

"Let's observe the scene of the crime," Victor said. "We'll get Kate and Ginny from the hotel, get a boat, and row down to where you found him. We can bring Denny and Lila and send them back with the boat so we can walk. See if we can figure out the path the man took from this house to his last resting place."

"Lila and Denny?"

"They came yesterday to London and joined us when we came down here. Denny says a day on the water would be welcome. Lila says we can't allow you to run amuck in Oxford without backup."

Violet shot him a look and then finished her letters to Hamilton and Jack.

"We need to talk to Nathan Tanner as well," she told him. "Find someone to hunt up the fellow. He said he was an assistant for...oh my, it was a unique name. A professor. Professor, umm...." Violet sniffed and then it came back to her. "Snag. I think if we can find him, we can find Tanner."

"Why does he matter?"

"I think he might answer questions," Violet told him. "Perhaps. Let's discover what we can about him; maybe he can be bribed to answer questions. He wasn't working directly with Mr. Morgan or these fellows anymore. He'd left after the death of Miss Morgan."

"Miss Morgan again?" Victor's brows lifted, but both of them shook heads at each other.

Miss Morgan had been dead long before this crime had committed. They were thinking like authors of light-hearted fiction again. Thankfully Jack wasn't there to roll his eyes or snort derisively.

Violet glanced around the room, rang the bell for the butler again, and handed off the notes. She thanked him for his assistance the last few days and left a monetary gift for the servants who'd taken care of her, especially the previous day. Being dumbfounded and alone, and having him step in had persuaded her to like him rather more than she might have otherwise.

She thanked him fervently, and they left.

CHAPTER ELEVEN

*M*r. Morgan's butler had taken the rooms that were available in the hotel, which was a rather large, opulent suite with four separate bedrooms, a dining area, and a sitting room in the center of the bedrooms. Kate rose as they entered. Violet hugged her fiercely.

"I missed you," Violet whispered, and then leaned down to scratch the soft ears of Gin and Rouge. Violet's dog was wiggling with unbounded joy at her presence.

"Did he propose?" Denny asked from across the room.

Victor answered before Violet could. "He did. The folks who found the body broke into the moment before Vi could answer."

"We're in the midst of a proposal rift?" Kate asked. She sounded quite sympathetic. "Poor Jack."

"Poor Violet," Vi countered.

"I don't know—" Lila's lips were twitching. "A proposal that is paused by a dead body is about perfect for these two. He couldn't have arranged it better. They met during a murder investigation—"

Violet winced, hating to think about losing her great aunt.

"Then, being separated by the murder of Isolde's horrific betrothed—"

Violet sighed.

"Both pulled farther apart and drawn back together by Tomas's hangers-on and the murder of that Bettina woman."

Violet crossed to a tea cart in the room, interrupting Lila's vocal recollection. She looked through it and happily poured herself a cup of Turkish coffee. Having only tea the last few days had been near torture. Mr. Morgan kept a traditional house and hadn't served any sort of coffee. What was wrong with the man? Violet sighed into her cup of coffee and took a seat.

"Are you ready for me to continue?" Lila's light voice took Violet's attention, and she glanced around at her friends, all of whom seemed too amused by the outcome of Violet's proposal. The body itself was unamusing, of course. The rest, however, did delight their evil sense of humor.

"Please," Violet said, knowing it would go faster if she just listened.

"Then, we shall continue to the most romantic of Christmas disasters when both of our young titans, Victor and Violet, were restored to love's path. Trodding through the crimes of others, they ended in a tropical vacation, dipped in rum, and showered in love. We see our heroes again in the backwoods of England, where their modern ways challenge the good folk of our fair country with their degenerate Jazz and drinking and roller-skating."

Violet lifted her cup in salute and sipped again, closing her eyes. "I much prefer you degenerates to Jack's stalwart Mr. Morgan."

"He doesn't appreciate your wit?"

"I believe he likes me well enough, but rather like you'd enjoy a dog or a clever little monkey. With a dash of derision and condescension. Hamilton is, of course, entirely different. He might be too responsible to be a daily member of our fair crew, but I think he should be an excellent occasional mascot."

Victor grunted as he sat down next to her.

"Where is Ginny?"

"She was taken on a tour of the town by her tutor, who is stalwart and true," Lila answered. "Determined to teach our sweet urchin Latin, the modern languages, music, and drawing."

Violet shot Lila a look, and she stopped describing the education of Victorian females.

"I suppose our grandmothers were not taught Latin," Lila admitted. She crossed her ankles. "I might have started with what I actually heard of the lessons and then become fanciful. Dare I suggest that Ginny seems to be learning?"

"Of course she is," Victor said. "Violet lectured her quite bluntly."

Violet's head tilted as she examined her brother. "Did you listen in on my conversations with *our* ward?" she demanded.

"Course I did," he said lazily. "You were grand. Epic. A lecture for the ages."

Violet gasped. "You could have assisted."

"But you had it so well in hand."

"She's failing out of school, Victor."

"You did wonderful." Victor winked at the others and then clapped softly for Violet.

Her eyes narrowed on him.

"You started with love. Made sure she knew you were on her side."

Violet began to set her coffee cup down and then thought better of it.

"You ignored her attempt to side-step the conversation with

that 'I prefer never' answer when you asked when she'd be prepared to talk about it."

Violet's fingernail tapped against the coffee cup with a sharp, click, click, click.

"And then," Victor said exultantly, "you were blunt and kind at the same time. Telling her she'd be unlikely to find her 'Lila' outside of school—"

"Ahhh," Lila cooed.

"While also telling her that doing well in school was the avenue to finding like-minded people."

"You," Violet didn't have the words. That had been one of the hardest conversations she'd ever had, the one she'd felt most ill-qualified for, and he'd...he'd...just left her to it.

"And then," Victor added with a happy grin, "my favorite part..."

Violet frowned fiercely as her fingernail continued to click, click, click.

"You promised you'd take care of the teachers who are being awful to her as well."

"What now?" Kate demanded. "The teachers?"

Violet and Victor nodded in the exact same way with the exact same tilt to their heads.

"You *will* be taking care of it, yes?" Kate's fury was clear and chilling.

"I believe it's Victor's turn at the bat."

He gasped and Violet grinned evilly at him. He winced. "Suddenly I feel rather like an idiot."

"So you should, my lad," Denny told him. "If you'd kept quiet until after Violet had handled it all, you could have tormented her and avoided all the work. Have a chocolate. It'll make you feel better." Denny lifted a box, but Victor waved it off.

"I need a cocktail for this," he muttered.

Violet sipped her coffee, the tapping of her nail having ceased with her revenge.

"Don't worry too much about it, boyo," Denny told him. "Kate will help you. This is why we marry. These ladies step up and take over, don't you know. Lads like us, we can go on doing nothing and being happy enough in our place just out of the gutters. The ladies ensure we have things like food and blankets and such. They're the most useful to have around."

Lila didn't even react to Denny's lazy comment any more than Kate or Violet.

"So, we're going to end this investigation, wrap up that proposal, and go wedding shopping, aren't we?" Kate asked.

"Sounds like a plan," Lila mused. "A boy dead in the river? Let's find the one who was stupid enough to commit murder."

"You're going to be involved this time?" Violet asked. "Last time you 'didn't want to.'"

"Last time," Lila replied, "my favorite love story wasn't half-finished. I simply had to finish the book."

"Hey now," Denny protested, and Lila arched her brow at him. He snuffled a little and shoved a chocolate into his mouth before he said around the sweet, "I suppose that's fair enough. We're old news, darling. Prosaic. Boring."

"Perhaps we should spice things up?" she asked him.

Denny considered for a moment, popped another chocolate into his mouth before answering. "We could. If you wanted. I guess. But that would probably interrupt our whole nap, dancing, drinks, nap cycle."

"A valid point, my love. A valid point."

～

The gents were sent off for boats while Violet arranged with the hotel for a picnic basket, several bottles of chilled lemon-ade, ginger beer, and champagne, and snacks enough for them and Hamilton and Jack. She felt certain the men would realize what they were up to before the day was out and hunt them up.

Violet grinned at Lila, who asked, "How angry do you think Jack will be?"

"It's not like he doesn't know Violet by now," Kate answered for Violet. "He and that war buddy, Scotland Yard brother of his are probably exchanging bets on which way she'll start to meddle."

Violet blinked, then grinned evilly. "Well, let's make sure they both lose."

"Indeed. Jack can't go getting lazy like Denny where you're concerned," Lila grinned and glanced at Kate. "Not before he even has you. He needs to...stretch a bit."

"And then fall to his knees like Victor did."

"Begging does look good on Victor," Violet told her future-sister-in-law. They gathered up the food, leaving the spaniels with Beatrice.

"There is a lad we need to find," Violet told them as they left the hotel. "Nathan Tanner. He was at the reception at the same time as Mr. Allen and the other lads."

"So, there's a boy?" Lila demanded.

Violet nodded. "He stole a photograph of his lost love, the tragically deceased Miss Morgan, from Mr. Morgan's house. I thought he might be the easiest mark to get a start on what nonsense is happening here. Aren't they supposed to be getting drunk, having private gambling dens in their rooms, and making alliances that will see them through the decades? Since when does university time end in murder?"

They walked through Oxford to the river, Violet explaining all that had happened since she arrived. They found the gents standing next to two rowboats as she finished.

"Is this where you and Jack left from?" Kate asked.

Violet stepped into the boat with Victor and Kate, and Lila and Denny took the second boat.

"No, we were farther upriver. I wasn't paying attention. Jack was acting different, and I was worried about the scandalous Miss Allen."

Lila chuckled when Violet mentioned Jack's behavior, and they all cast Violet a look.

"For such a clever girl, you'd think she'd have realized what Jack was up to," Victor said to them all. "I certainly can never get anything past you," he said to Violet, "unless I'm full on hiding in the hallway like I was during your talk with our sweet Ginny."

Violet leaned back, adjusting her hat as she said, "Well, get on with it, my lad."

Victor grunted as Violet made it apparent that she, at least, would not be helping with the boat. Her eyes were fixed on the greenery around the river as she examined the riverbanks. There were others on the river, but Violet paid them little attention.

"There," she pointed, and Victor moved the boat towards where she directed. They rowed for a while down the side of the river where Jeremiah's body was found. Violet was on her knees, balancing as she examined the riverbank. It took a good amount of time for Violet's attention to be grabbed. But there, on the green beyond the riverbank, the perfect verdant lawn was broken by streaks of mud. It was apparent that something had happened near the river just there. Once they made shore, Violet stepped out, using Victor's hand to leap from the boat onto the green. She walked down the riverside. Much of it was bound in by stone and walks, but it seemed an argument could have happened at this location.

Or perhaps boys had been wrestling on their holidays, and there was nothing sinister in this patch of ruined grass. There wasn't much of a reason to believe that it had been Mr. Allen and his killer other than the marks looked fresh and it was close to where Mr. Allen's body was found the evening before. It was also upriver. If Mr. Allen had gone into the river near here, it would make sense that he floated downstream for a ways before he was caught in the reeds.

She sighed and turned back to the boat. "This could be anything. We're treading water with no reason to go any direction."

Lila's lips twitched from her place in the boat while Denny's gaze was fixed behind Violet. She turned, meeting the penetrating, dark gaze of the man she loved. He was frowning ferociously at her. Violet tried for an innocent expression, but it was too much to hope he'd believe her.

"Ah, Violet," Hamilton said from beside him. "I assumed we'd discover you at some point today. Jack said, however, it would be sooner rather than later. You have lost me a bottle of my favorite wine."

Lila's laugh broke through the staring contest between Violet and Jack. She winked at him and said, "Looks like Vi wasn't wrong about there being a dustup between poor Mr. Allen and his killer. The lads have got it. I suppose we'll have to eat this cold chicken and fruit all alone. Unless—"

Lila held up the basket invitingly, and Hamilton glanced at Jack before he crossed to the boat. "We have to eat, lad. Ruminate. We won't be able to think without sustenance."

"We have ginger beer," Violet offered. Her own extreme love for ginger beer and wine had infected Jack, who sighed, but he led them farther up the green, away from the possible scene of the crime.

Violet allowed Jack to take her hand and help seat her, then she watched as Jack returned to help Victor pull the boat onto the shore. They opened the picnic baskets and began serving the food. Violet noticed a lump in Jack's coat pocket, and she leaned forward, winding her arm around his elbow and taking a moment to try to peek inside. It was an oval frame such as might have fit a small space on a mantel. She felt a flash of guilt for not explaining about the missing photograph most likely in Mr. Tanner's pocket, but then again—

She grinned at him and leaned her chin onto his shoulder, promising she'd tell him later that day.

They were working through the chicken and grapes as Jack stared around them. A bridge was nearby, and Jack's gaze fixed on it.

"Do you think?"

He was speaking to Hamilton but Violet answered. "If it was a fraught enough fight, he might have run that way."

Hamilton grunted an agreement and drained his bottle of ginger beer. "I'd have run that way. Hoped to find help near the bridge. Lost the battle over the water."

Jack finished the thought. "He could have easily either been thrown into the water with that blow on his head, or the blow could have knocked the boy into the river. If he were unconscious—"

"He'd have died certainly," Vi finished for him. "How long until they know if he went in alive or dead?"

Jack and Hamilton didn't answer, and Violet assumed they already knew. Her gaze flitted to Kate and Lila.

"They already know," Lila told Violet.

"And they're protecting you," Kate added.

"Which means," Violet started.

"He's protecting you," Victor finished. "The foolish lads. They need training yet. Not all the fellows have such excellent pre-training as myself. You have saved Kate a world of trouble."

Jack tossed Hamilton a long-suffering look, and then sighed as he stood. "It was delightful, Vi. All of Vi's minions." He leaned down and pressed a kiss to her forehead, letting his fingers trail across the back of her neck. He squeezed lightly then left.

CHAPTER TWELVE

"*M*iss Allen or Mr. Tanner?" Violet rose, setting her napkin into the basket and returning her empty bottle of ginger beer to the basket.

"I would normally excuse myself for a nap during the heat of the day," Lila declared, adjusting her hair. She waved her fan lazily, barely causing a breeze as though the cooling air wasn't enough to propel her to greater action. "I would, however, very much like to meet this Miss Allen. Do we know where she's staying?"

Violet's brows lifted. "It's not as though we are the best of friends, or that we have a standing appointment for tea."

"Well," Kate said, "it can't be all that hard, can it? She's rich enough that people suspect her brother bought his way into that program he was part of. She isn't going to be at a fleabag hotel. Chances are she's at the place where we're staying. Or one that Mr. Morgan's butler inquired about. Send Beatrice or Giles to the butler to ask if he knows where she is. If he does, ask which hotel and send round your card."

Violet considered Kate's statement. Hamilton and Jack

certainly knew where Miss Allen was staying. Someone had told her that her brother had died. They weren't going to tell her.

Violet tapped her finger against her palm. She'd already left a nice monetary reward for the staff, but they could pull a Victor and send over a bottle of gin or rum to Mr. Morgan's people. It was very like Violet to send chocolates. Either or both or all of it, whatever it took to persuade the staff to be generous with their information.

Violet agreed, and they meandered through Oxford until they reached the high-ceilinged hotel. The walls were thick and the foyer floors marble and stone, which gave an illusion of coolness. As soon as one adjusted to the seeming coolness, the heat hit again.

Kate sent for Beatrice to have cool lemonade brought to their rooms. Victor followed after Kate as he usually did, with Lila joining them.

"Jack kissed you before he left," Denny said on the lift. The lift attendant carefully avoided reacting in any way.

"Did you save that comment for when we'd have an audience?"

Denny grinned in reply. "But he did."

"Mmm," Violet agreed.

"I wonder if he assumes you'll answer yes."

"He doesn't get to assume anything," Violet replied. "I'm Lady Violet Carlyle until I tell him otherwise."

Denny hooted in reply. The lift stopped and Violet inclined her head at the attendant as she left. They made their way back to their suite, and Violet walked in and spun around.

"Ginny?"

There was no answer.

"She must still be gone," Denny replied. "The good news is that she won't be here to witness you causing trouble for your beloved. Maybe you can keep up the pretense of being a good example when she returns."

Violet spun slowly on Denny, who held up his hands in surrender while also grinning at her.

"This is what comes of being friends with idiots."

Denny's low chuckle was a clear agreement.

The door to their suite opened a few minutes later to admit Lila, Kate, and Victor.

"Darling Vi," Victor called, "Kate was right. She's here in this hotel. Did you want to...I mean...what is the right way to handle this?"

"Send Giles to find out about Mr. Nathan Tanner as soon as he returns. We'll talk to him next. I have discovered a rather fierce need to speak with him since seeing Jack."

"You should do that thing," Denny said. "That thing with the list and the names and the brainwork. It makes me feel quite faint just thinking about it, but I believe we can all agree that you have greater mettle than do I."

Violet shot him an irritated glance as sweet little Rouge placed a paw on her knee. Violet reached forward and scratched the little ruby head.

"I suppose if I must," she answered Denny.

"You must," Denny said. "It's my favorite part."

"Me pacing?"

"You pacing. It makes me feel as though I'm helping. I'm ah... willing you on."

"Willing me on?"

Violet glanced over and saw that Beatrice had entered. "Please bring my journal. Though, Denny, we really must speak with Miss Allen and Tanner before we can start that business. Who are we going to put on our list now? Every person at the university who found Mr. Allen annoying? Miss Allen, who was trying to save her brother?"

"Of course! I prefer the sideways mysteries with the one you'd have never expected as the killer. The older sister who seemingly is out to save the young blighter but is only securing the inheritance for herself."

Lila sat down next to her husband, patting his hand. "Better cut that off, my lad. The sister has been invited up for tea."

"It's too hot for tea," Denny whined. "It's nap time. I need my beauty sleep."

"Buck up, laddie," Lila declared. She brushed the hair back from his face and then scratched behind his ear rather as Violet was doing for Rouge.

"Where is Gin?" Violet asked suddenly, watching Lila treat her husband like a dog.

"He's sleeping in my bedroom," Victor replied. "He rather likes my socks drawer. If we're going to play nice with Jack's old fiancé, I need to make my tea with whiskey before she gets here. I don't think I can handle being kind any other way. We all know Jack, don't we? He'd never have thrown her over. She must have done it."

Violet didn't answer, idly scratching Rouge's head instead. There was a knock on the door and Victor swore as he said, "That had better be the tea and lemonade Kate ordered."

It was Miss Allen. Her lush beauty had not diminished, but Violet saw the dark circles under Miss Allen's honey brown eyes.

"My condolences on your brother," Violet said.

"Spare me your lies," Miss Allen snapped. "If you cared so much about my brother, you'd have helped me."

Violet's expression remained even.

"Here now," Victor started, but Violet held up her hand.

"As if you could even understand," Miss Allen said maliciously.

Violet's fingers crossed in her lap. Twice over, to be exact. Miss Allen knew that Violet had lost brothers in the war, and Vi was hardly going to use her brothers in any way. Peter and Lionel deserved better from her.

"I assume," Violet said, "that you came because you want help in finding your brother's killer."

"That's what Jack is for," Miss Allen said sharply. "He feels responsible for Jeremy's death. I don't need *you* to investigate when I have him, let alone my own talents."

Those words were put together in such a way to hurt Violet, but again, Violet would not give Miss Allen the pleasure of showing that hurt.

There was a knock on the door of the suite, and Kate rose to let in the tea.

"Ah," Violet said smoothly, channeling her stepmother, "the tea has arrived. How lovely." She turned her attention back to Miss Allen. "Did you assume that you could somehow use whatever Jack might feel about your brother as an avenue to restoring what you once had with him?"

"I am only here as a warning for you to let him go," Miss Allen said. She tilted her head as she added, "Did you really think that you'd be able to keep his attention? The spoiled daughter of an earl who writes tripe? The only thing you can offer is money, and Jack has enough. Should he wish more, I can give it to him." Miss Allen's gaze flicked over Violet and found her clearly wanting. "I read your *Broken Surrender and the Scarlet Ghost*. It was *terrible*."

"As entertaining as this is," Victor cut in, not even trying to hide his disgust or the healthy dollop of whiskey in his tea. "Let's stop posturing, ladies. I won't bother to tell you that you have no chance with Jack, and Violet will avoid telling you that she's not responsible because she didn't respond as you wish to your ham-handed attempt to blackmail us."

"For you," Miss Allen, said, turning her spite on him, "all of this is a lark. For a woman, it's different. Isn't it, *Lady Vi?*"

Violet examined the woman across from her. "I understand you being jealous. I understand finding comfort in him being the one to investigate your brother's case, especially the combination of Jack and Hamilton. I understand disliking me—after all, I'd never have had a chance for Jack's love if you hadn't killed his love for you. But..."

Miss Allen lifted a perfectly sculpted brow and pursed her perfectly lush lips, watching Violet.

"But what I don't understand," Vi continued, "is why you're here if that's your whole truth."

"So we're playing it entirely straightforward, are we?"

"You're a reporter," Violet said. "You're either setting us on a goose chase for the fun of it, or you know as well as we do that the police and official investigators come at a problem one way, and we *girls* come at it another."

Miss Allen hadn't lost the sheen of grief in her eyes as she nodded once, but her lips twitched with a humor that none of them felt. She moved to sit across from Violet.

"He wanted to be like Jack." Miss Allen's voice cracked. "He never quite forgave me for ruining things between us. I stole his mentor from him, the brother he always wanted, his hero."

Violet sympathized with Miss Allen. Violet could imagine that he would have hated her for losing Jack for the both of them.

"What do you truly want from me, Miss Allen?"

Miss Allen took in a deep breath and held it, then released it. "I want my brother's killer found. I would have thought that he was wrong about his theory. Surely one of his wild theories was the reason he was killed. He was bumbling through his *investigation*. He was making enemies. But he couldn't have been all wrong. Not if he died." She pursed her lips as though admitting the next was distasteful. "You're right about Jack following the investigation according to their procedures. He isn't going to just follow his instincts. Not directly. You, me, we follow our instincts, and we do things like ignore the law for the story."

Violet glanced at Victor.

"You owe me," Miss Allen insisted.

"No, Emily, I do not owe you. I am not responsible for your brother's bumbling nor am I the killer. I have no obligations to you. But I will help you. We all will."

"I won't," Lila said as she sipped from her glass of lemonade. "I don't care. I got what I wanted."

"I was never actually going to help." Denny dug through the tea tray for the biscuits and sighed happily when he found them. He grinned at his wife and saluted her with the biscuits.

"You are not eating that whole tray," Lila told him, ignoring Emily.

"You are all idiots," Emily declared. "By Jove! How does Jack stand you?"

Violet smirked, and Kate laughed outright.

Victor simply leaned back and crossed his legs as he sipped his tea. "I'm going to have to talk to Jack again. My faith in him is trembling after meeting Miss Allen."

"Come now," Denny said. "How many men do you know who've fallen for snakes like this one? He probably realized what she was like before she dumped him and took the betrayal with relief."

Jack had said he'd been broken. By this woman? There must be something more to her. Violet examined the beautiful Emily again, taking in the sadness on her face. Perhaps there was a heart in the woman? Something that Jack had once held and treasured? Violet didn't need Jack to tell her it was so, and the jealousy she'd managed to avoid so far hit her full throttle. She reached out and took her brother's teacup. This type of feeling needed a hard dose of whiskey, though she'd have preferred to have it without the tea.

Miss Allen pulled a journal from her satchel, handed it to Violet, and said, "My brother deserves a champion even if I don't." She rose with an elegance and grace that Violet hadn't been aware she was lacking and nodded at the room in general before leaving.

"Well, that was convenient," Victor said before Miss Allen had even left the rooms. "I don't trust her."

"We should definitely put her on the top of your suspect list, Vi," Denny added, grabbing a biscuit from the tray as Lila reached to move it. Beatrice closed the door behind Jack's former fiancé while Violet finished off Victor's tea-flavored whiskey.

Vi flipped through the journal. "Beatrice, go to Mr. Morgan's house. Tell Jack we need his assistance. Tell him whatever he needs to hear including about Miss Allen and what she said here."

"Are we making your list yet, Vi? Please say you're putting Miss Allen at the top of it?"

Violet glanced at Denny, who was slouched in the most comfortable of the chairs. He popped the last of his biscuit in his mouth and smiled lazily at his wife.

"I wonder if she's an only child now," Victor said. "If someone killed you, I'd be at the top of the list."

"Nah," Violet countered. "Isolde is my heir."

CHAPTER THIRTEEN

*V*iolet didn't leave the rooms since she had sent for Mr. Tanner and Jack. They were the ones who could help. She started the list of suspects, but she didn't have enough information to make suspects. She could list off everyone who had been at the reception for Hamilton Barnes, but most of them neither knew nor cared to know a first-year university student who was only invited to the reception because of his father's money.

Violet rose, giving Victor back his emptied teacup. What could she do for her list? Write down the blonde one? The red-headed one? It was ridiculous. But...

"Kate, would you take notes?"

Violet didn't even look, knowing Kate would help.

"Mr. Morgan has to be a suspect," Violet said. "Jeremiah might have worked for him, but we have no idea what the young Mr. Allen truly thought of Morgan."

Violet heard the scratch of Kate's pen on the paper.

"Nathan Tanner is my second suspect after Emily Allen."

Violet fiddled with her ring as she paced. It was hot in the rooms. "After this business is finished, we're going to the sea, yes? We should write to Isolde and Gerald and ask them to meet us in Lyme or Bath or somewhere with sea air to go with the British soil. Seeing that *woman* Emily lose her brother makes me miss them."

"I'll write to them," Victor told her.

Violet glanced at her twin. "We really should beg them to come home. If Lady Eleanor finds out about our alter ego, having Isolde around to distract her mother might be just the thing."

"Violet! Brilliant!"

Lila laughed softly as Victor begged more paper from Kate. "Is that Emily really your first suspect?"

Violet shook her head, and then tilted it as she considered more fully. "We have to have faith in Jack. He might have made a mistake in her. But a mistake to the level of loving someone who would kill her brother? It's too easy. Her presence here feels... convenient for the murderer."

"But he thought he loved her. Maybe he isn't as clever as we think," Victor said doubtfully, but his eyes were glinting with humor, and Violet knew he was teasing her. "Maybe he took so long asking you to marry him because of that? Are you still going to say yes?"

"I haven't given anyone my answer, *twin.*"

"She says it like it's a curse," Denny laughed.

"I am a pearl of great price," Victor said, using one of Violet's favorite quotes.

"You're going to say yes, Violet," Lila added, crossing to the collection of bottles that Giles had unpacked. "We already know it."

"You don't know anything," Violet said. "Let's return to the list at hand, please."

"So you want to put this poor Mr. Tanner on the list. Why?"

"We return," Violet answered, "to the beloved innocent, Rachael Morgan. Hamilton mentioned on the train that Jeremiah thought there was a murder; so did Emily when she was trying to blackmail me. It seems unlikely that there was another odd death outside of the young woman's"

"This isn't a novel, Vi," Victor sighed.

"No, but she *is* dead and Jeremiah felt a crime had been committed. The younger Mr. Tanner was certainly in love with her. If her death was suspicious then Tanner is a suspect."

"How are you certain?" Kate asked, without stopping her notes.

"He stole a photograph that was likely of her from Mr. Morgan's. At the time, I had thought it was romantic and sad. Like Romeo and Juliet."

Victor snorted. "A little communication between those two would have been far more romantic than the poison and the blade."

Violet's expression became long-suffering, and she glanced at Kate. "Thus with a kiss I die."

"Would have been far more romantic to go to sleep in each other's arms and wake for a hearty breakfast, in my opinion," Denny said through a yawn.

"No one asked you, my lad," Lila told him. "It was romantic."

"It was stupid," Victor countered.

"It was fiction," Kate said, shaking her head. "Neither Juliet nor Romeo lived and they did not die from poison or a blade. It was the cruel stroke of a pen and nothing more. Perhaps we should return our attention to the tragedy at hand rather than our petty squabbles."

"For another day," Denny said, yawning again. "On another day, Victor and I would have been victorious."

Lila's snort was his only answer.

"So he took a photograph of the dead girl from the house." Kate wrote it down, but she looked up after she finished. "Why does that make her death suspicious?"

"Because," Violet said, "Jack had the photograph in his pocket today. When we found them searching for the scene of the crime, he'd already discovered the photograph. Mr. Tanner was either there or he had given the photograph to Jeremiah Allen before he died. I didn't tell Jack I saw the boy steal the photograph. I thought it was romantic, and I didn't want to get Tanner in trouble if Jack decided to tell Morgan."

"You saw the photograph in Jack's pocket and didn't say anything about how it came to be missing?" Victor's voice conveyed his opinion, and Violet winced.

"I should have said something." She ran her fingers through her hair, wincing at her own stupidity. She had sent Beatrice for Jack because Violet knew she had made a mistake. It would have been incurably stupid of her to approach a man who was the *like-liest* suspect in this investigation, given that if Mr. Allen was correct, the killer had both killed Miss Morgan and then Mr. Allen to hide his crime.

Perhaps Violet's guess about Rachael Morgan was wrong. It could have been another crime that Mr. Allen was tripping into. His sister referenced multiple investigations. Except, Violet thought, you didn't necessarily commit murder to hide petty thievery or plagiarism or even blackmail. The punishment for murder was too great when compared to nearly anything else.

Violet fiddled with her ring, worried that Jack wouldn't forgive her. She paced back and forth before the windows, hoping that Beatrice would be successful in tracking down Jack and Hamilton.

The telephone in the suite rang, and Victor answered it while

Violet's attention was caught by the journal Miss Allen had left. She crossed to it.

A part of her wished to hand it over to Jack as amends, and a part of her wanted to keep it for herself and use whatever she might learn to solve this crime. The reason she was helping—or meddling—was because Violet didn't want to carry the guilt of not helping Mr. Allen. Especially when Jack had to be carrying the same guilt—his guilt tinged with memories of the young man as a boy and being the subject of hero worship.

Violet winced for Jack and looked up when the suite door opened. It was Ginny and her tutor. It took Lila a long-suffering minute before she stood and said, "Come along you two. We're off."

"But we just got back," Ginny protested, her gaze flicking to Violet.

"We'll go have tea," Lila ordered, "and then go shopping. I very much look forward to giving your dear Victor a bill for a slew of nonsense."

"Get more chocolates, darling," Denny said before rising and going to their bedroom. Violet had no doubt that Denny would be asleep in the next few minutes.

Lila grabbed her handbag, shot Violet a look and left. As they did, they passed Jack in the doorway. He watched Lila leave with the girl and her tutor and then turned to the others.

"What's going on?"

"We've lost faith in you," Victor proclaimed, rising to pour himself another drink and making one for Jack as well. "We've met the horror."

"The horror?" Jack asked, looking to Violet for a translation.

"Miss Allen is staying in this hotel. We had a visit with her." It took Violet a moment to decide. "Here." She pushed the journal at him. "Emily said that this contains her brother's notes on whatever he was investigating. He must have given her details about what he was investigating since she tried to blackmail me into getting you to help. Perhaps after the train and before the reception. I am guessing since she handed the journal over, he doesn't clarify which of his theories were the aim of his focus before he died."

Jack glanced down at the leather-bound journal and then around the room. Kate and Victor were both staring at poor Jack.

"You called her Emily? You're on a first names basis now?"

"I got tired of Miss Allen," Violet told him. "She was using 'lady' so ironically, I countered as I could."

Jack grunted and sat down. He lifted the drink that Victor had poured and looked at it for a moment before shrugging and taking a sip. "She's a viper," Jack muttered.

"Oh thank goodness," Kate said, taking a drink from Victor. "I was so worried that you weren't nearly as clever as we'd thought."

"Believe me—" Jack took another long sip of whatever Victor had poured. He sighed. "I doubted myself for some time after I was free. I think Ham still has a celebratory drink on the anniversary of things falling apart."

Victor handed Violet a glass of ginger wine and she smiled into it.

"I could drink to that," Victor told Jack, clapping him on the shoulder.

"You could drink to anything," Kate said, setting aside her drink and looking down at her notes. "Get it over with, Violet. Before we're interrupted again."

Violet met Jack's gaze, saw it sharpen on her, and sipped her comforting wine.

"Are we expecting company?" Jack's head tilted as they stared at each other. He didn't look angry that she was still here. He didn't seem angry that he'd found them searching out the site of the dispute. He did know what he was getting with Violet, she thought. She didn't surprise him at all.

"Nathan Tanner is coming. We've invited him."

"Should I be concerned by your interest in some university lad?"

"He was the one who took that photograph of Rachael Morgan at the reception last night. I don't know how you found it today, but I assume it has something to do with what happened to Jeremiah."

Given the expression on Jack's face, Violet felt it was a good thing he'd set his drink down. He looked as though he'd have choked on it. He examined the journal she'd given him and then shook his head. "How do you find these things out?"

"He was interesting at the reception. I was bored."

Jack reached out and took her hand, rubbing his thumb over her wrist. "You would be an excellent detective. You knew there was something wrong while the rest of us were making small talk about the weather and whatever laurels we had to prose on about."

Violet wove their fingers together as she looked at the journal in his lap. "I'd like to help."

"I'd like you to be safe."

"I won't go anywhere without Victor or you."

"People will tell her things that they don't tell you, Jack," Kate told him. "You're intimidating. They all think she's nothing but fluff, cocktails, and money. Half the men who meet her think about how great it would be if they were you. They all seem to believe they have a chance at her because she is almost as good as Victor at hiding her cleverness."

Victor snorted at Kate's backhanded compliment.

"Don't take it as accolades, luv. My life would be far easier if my mother thought you were clever about anything other than cocktails."

"I'm quite good at twinning," Victor pronounced. "Tell your mother that one. That'll get her on my side."

"Let us help?" Violet asked Jack quietly. "It's not necessary, you know. To do this alone. I think, if Mr. Tanner isn't the killer, that he might talk to me."

Jack's face searched hers, and she tried a winning smile. He grinned at her when she pasted the dopey expression on her face. "You won't approach them alone? You promise?"

"I promise." Violet crossed her fingers over her heart and fluttered her lashes at him. He shook his head as another telephone call came from the front desk. Victor answered it and a moment later said, "He's on his way up."

CHAPTER FOURTEEN

"Kate, pretend as though you are writing a letter in the corner and take notes. Victor, quickly make Tanner a drink and then eavesdrop from one of the bedrooms with Jack. Beatrice, take the dogs into one of the other bedrooms."

They scattered according to Violet's instructions, and Violet stopped Jack at the knock on the door. "May I have Mr. Allen's journal?"

Jack hesitated and then handed it to Violet, who tossed it haphazardly on one of the chairs in plain view. She grinned at him and then winked, shooing him away as she turned, but before Jack let her step away, he took her wrist and pulled her close to him. His fingers pressed into her lower spine with one hand while the other continued to shackle her wrist. With a low voice that only Violet could hear, he leaned in, nuzzling his chin over her forehead and said, "We will find a time to finish our earlier conversation."

There was no question to which conversation he referred and

Violet shivered. She wanted a re-do on that proposal without interruptions and without the flavor of Miss Allen and her brother tainting the moment.

"When this is done," she said and slipped from his hands to open the door to the suite. Jack stepped through the open doorway where Victor had already disappeared as Violet greeted their guest.

"Mr. Tanner," she said, as he shuffled before her. "Thank you so much for coming."

He shrugged and entered when she stepped back for him.

Violet examined him. He'd left with a photograph that ended up with the dead body. Why? What had happened since he left Morgan's house to now?

"I thought you were staying with Mr. Morgan."

"I was," Violet told him lightly, channeling the cheery voice she used whenever the occasion called for it. "Did you hear of the awful accident that befell Mr. Jeremiah Allen? My friends are doing what they can, and I didn't want to be a bother to Mr. Morgan while they were gone. It's hardly fair to invite someone for a day and have them linger on. Not comfortable for any of us really." She gestured to Kate and lowered her voice. "My friend is in the middle of writing quite a terrible letter. Her mother is... well...I'm sure you have difficult people in your life. She probably won't even realize you're here. I'd interrupt her, but..." Violet leaned in confidentially, "She's been working on that letter for hours. I'm rather terrified to stop the flow of her thoughts and have her turn on me. She's got a bit of a gorgon in her when thwarted."

Mr. Tanner smiled, but like in their last conversation, it didn't reach his eyes. "What can I do for you, Lady Violet? Your invitation was rather unexpected."

Violet gestured him to a seat and handed him a drink that

Victor had poured heavy and strong. It probably wouldn't loosen the tongue of a university student who had probably developed the ability to drink to an excess, but Violet thought they might as well try.

She sat down across from Mr. Tanner and asked, "Then why did you come?"

"Why wouldn't I?" His gaze shifted to the side as he answered, and Violet guessed she knew the reason why.

"You took that photograph from Mr. Morgan's home and wondered if I had seen you. It must be all the more fraught since you've lost it."

Mr. Tanner froze as though a ghost had walked over his grave. He tried to laugh it off, but he choked on the laughter. "I—"

"I'd prefer that you aren't the killer of Mr. Allen or Miss Morgan," Violet said quietly, and if Kate weren't paying attention she might not have heard.

"I—"

"I'd prefer to believe that my first reading of you, that of the heartbroken young man, was accurate. Was it?"

"I..."

Violet searched his face. With his ginger coloring and paler skin, the flush on his neck, ears, and cheeks was all the more powerful.

"Mr. Tanner," Violet said gently. "Tell me about it. Let me help you."

"Why would you help me?" His tone was agonized, and he pushed his hands into his hair, leaning forward.

"Mr. Tanner, I should like to believe that a man who is mourning, as I can see that you are, is not the slayer of his beloved."

"She didn't...she wasn't...there's no reason to believe that anything happened to her that was nefarious. No reason except the incoherent ramblings of a young fool."

Violet believed him. Stupid though it may be, she believed him. She reached out and took his hand, turning it over, and placed the cocktail in it. He needed a stiff drink. He was going to need it desperately when she helped him process the next round of facts.

"There wasn't," Violet agreed. "I imagine that Mr. Morgan has enough official friends that they'd have stepped in to help if there was reason to believe she was murdered."

"Exactly," Mr. Tanner ground out. "Just what I told that fool Allen."

"If there was a scrap of reason to believe it, they would have found it. Those police officers and doctors. They would have stood up for Miss Morgan—the beloved niece of someone like Daniel Morgan."

"Yes!"

"By Jove," Violet added, building her argument purposefully but in careful measure. She was using the theory that the girl had been murdered because she was young and beautiful and it would have been a plot device if she were writing a book. A girl who had decided to love an unapproved man—of course she would die in a fluffy little book. She would die and send the hero on his quest. Violet added, "It would be ridiculous to think that a girl who was so widely beloved as Miss Morgan could be killed anyway. It wasn't as though she were doing something that would upset her family."

Mr. Tanner did not answer that one, and Violet's head tilted as she examined him once again. He hadn't reacted to what Violet had insinuated, but he knew that Miss Morgan's innocence was not as perfect as one might guess.

"Was she an heiress? Mr. Morgan's home feels quite a bit nicer than most professors would have."

Mr. Tanner nodded, his jaw trembling.

"Miss Morgan was lovely. That much is clear. Both in body and in her nature. Even the servants mourn her still."

Mr. Tanner nodded again, his lips trembling as he tried to hold back his emotions. That stiff British upper lip really was too difficult in times like these. These poor gents and their need to uphold their ideas of masculinity. This was a man who needed a good cry. Violet and Kate could both explain it to him, but he wouldn't give in.

Violet glanced at Kate, who was watching with open mouth.

"Mr. Tanner, I would have made that same argument to young Allen myself if he'd told me his worries."

"See?" Mr. Tanner cursed as he muttered, "Why did he have to make it linger on and on? Why couldn't he just let his theory go and let her rest in peace?"

Violet's voice was gentle when she answered that question. "Because he wasn't wrong."

Mr. Tanner dropped his glass onto the carpet and then apologized profusely.

"Don't let that worry you," she told him.

His gaze met hers, and his eyes were wide, his expression sick. "Why would you say that? Why would you say that about Rachael?"

Violet nibbled at her bottom lip and told herself that hesitating was only hurting him further.

"Because, Mr. Tanner, Mr. Allen was murdered."

Mr. Tanner paled, making the dark circles under his eyes and the flush on his cheeks all the more dramatic. "What?"

"Mr. Allen was murdered. The problem for you is that Miss Morgan, the heiress, loved you. Scholarship lad, I believe?"

Mr. Tanner nodded.

"Her uncle wouldn't have liked it, I think."

Mr. Tanner's hands were shaking, but he didn't answer.

"He wanted her to marry a student of his," Jack said from the doorway.

Mr. Tanner gasped and turned an accusatory gaze on Violet.

"That student wouldn't have been you. Daniel is many things, but he is an incurable snob."

"You're here with that Barnes fellow," Mr. Tanner said. "The one from Scotland Yard?"

"I am," Jack said neatly. "Come now, my man. Let us help you."

"Why would you help me? Why aren't you calling for the police right now?"

"Because Lady Violet Carlyle is far more clever than she'd have you believe. And she believes you're innocent."

Violet's gaze was fixed on Jack, but she could feel Mr. Tanner's on her. "Is that true? Lady Violet, do you think I am innocent?"

Violet nodded, facing Mr. Tanner. "Help us so we can help you."

"How?"

"Who did Mr. Allen believe killed Miss Morgan?"

"He didn't know. She declined rather suddenly at the end, but it was slow at first. She was a little paler each day. Then one day, she simply didn't wake up."

"What did Mr. Allen think had killed her?"

"Her tea," Mr. Tanner said, biting his lip. "She had this special mix. Black teas made her heart race, so she'd drink a blend of mint and berry teas. She loved it and special ordered it, and she was the only who drank it. She had it daily. If you wanted to kill her, it would have been easy to poison that tea and let her slowly die."

"You didn't believe him?"

"Her heart raced if she exercised too much. If she ran, if she had black teas. I loved her, Lady Violet, but Rachael wasn't strong. Her decline was horrible, but it also wasn't all that surprising."

"I remember that tea," Jack said. "Daniel had it mixed for her when she was still in the schoolroom. She didn't go off to school like the other girls because he worried over her. He had tutors in to teach her whatever she wanted to learn. Jeremy was right. It would have been easy to kill Rachael that way. Easy and nearly undetectable. We all knew she was delicate. Everyone who knew Daniel very well knew he was worried for her."

Violet rose to pace while Jack examined Nathan Tanner. He was young, and this was a terrible burden. He'd be all right with time, Violet thought. Her gaze, however, was on Jack. If Jack could come home from the war and restart his life, not once, but twice after Miss Allen, then Nathan Tanner could move past this.

As though he read her thoughts and understood them, he rose from his seat. "I watched her *die*. I thought her health was finally failing her, and I watched her die."

Violet had no idea what to say to that.

"I made peace with it," Mr. Tanner said in a hoarse whisper. "As much as you could, I did. I told her I would always love her. I told her I would never forget her. I promised her that I would love again. I thought she was too good to live. I thought God had taken her home because she was an angel. I...that...oh bloody hell..." Mr. Tanner stood again, moving rapidly across the room as though chased by the hounds of hell. He spun, staring at the two of them as they looked on his pain, and then he slammed his fist into the wall over and over again.

Violet jumped with each sound of his hand striking the wall, but she bit her lip to hold back objections. If he couldn't cry, he had to process what he was feeling somehow. Violet, however, could cry for him. The tears came in a steady stream by the time that Mr. Tanner had stopped beating the wall. He pressed his face into it, breathing heavily. Great gasps filled the room as he struggled to gather himself.

Finally, he spoke, his face still pressed into the wall. "I would have preferred to believe God took her home. I...I always knew it wouldn't be all that long with her. I always knew if we wed as we hoped that the clock was ticking away for her. I would have savored our time together. I would have made her happy. I would have loved her so fiercely she would have carried it with her to heaven."

"She did," Violet told him gently. "Of course she did."

He didn't answer, but he slowly turned. He was so pale, he'd gone from white to ghostly.

"I...want to help. I'll do whatever it takes to catch this person."

"You'll stay here," Jack told him. "You're at risk until we figure this out. Victor will get you a room. Victor!"

"Consider it taken care of," Victor said, as he came through the doorway. He crossed to Kate, pulled her to her feet, and drew her out of the room with him.

"Let's start with what Jeremy told you," Jack said to him, taking a seat again and waiting while Mr. Tanner collected himself enough to move back to the chair and sit. He had gone, Violet thought, from a whimpering rabbit who was struggling to carry on, to a coiled tiger. They would have to find the killer before Mr. Tanner did. Otherwise, Violet would find herself at odds with Jack when she helped another killer to escape justice.

CHAPTER FIFTEEN

"We all loved her." Mr. Tanner spoke when Violet was ready to believe he wouldn't speak at all. His voice was hoarse.

Violet couldn't help but reach for Jack at the pain in Mr. Tanner's voice. She held onto his hand as though she could keep someone from stealing him away like Miss Morgan had been taken from poor Mr. Tanner.

"I never understood why she loved me," he continued. "Elijah is quite eloquent. He's rich. Charming. He adored her. He used to write her poems, and by Jove, they were good."

"He was the one Daniel wanted her to marry, I think," Jack said.

It seemed as though Mr. Tanner wasn't going to reply, but he finally nodded jerkily. "Professor Morgan is quite fond of Elijah. We all are, to be honest. I am still baffled by her loving me over him. Sometimes, at night, I play it through my head. Remembering and wondering if I have somehow painted a fairy dream that wasn't true. If I am misremembering the sound of her voice promising to love me even in heaven. That can't be true? Can it? What is there to love about me?"

Violet wanted to ask questions, but it sounded as though the story was being ripped from his soul.

"If Jeremy's guess about the tea was right," Mr. Tanner said, gathering himself, "and you rule out the professor and the servants, it could have been any of us who were his research assistants. That would be me, Jeremiah—even though he was just a hanger-on—Elijah, Theodore, and Alexander."

Violet pressed her lips together to hold back her questions, but she didn't quite manage it. "There were no others who were there often? A secretary or other professors?"

"Well, Professor Snag works with Professor Morgan quite a bit. He is often there. Or was. He was often there *then*. They had an article they were working on together. I..." Mr. Tanner ran his hands over his face. "I suppose there were a few more of the boys who were around then. They've since graduated."

"They don't matter," Violet told him.

"They could have put the poison in Rachael's tea."

"But they wouldn't have killed Jeremiah if they're no longer in Oxford."

Mr. Tanner blinked a little stupidly before clarity came over his expression. "I suppose I really only care about Rachael's murder. Does that make me a villain?"

"It makes you a man in love," Jack told him. "Understandable."

"I thought to join Scotland Yard someday." He laughed derisively. "Scotland Yard? When the woman I love was killed under my watch and I didn't even realize what losing Allen meant."

"You are very young in investigating," Jack told him.

"Lady Violet saw it," Tanner said, shaking his head.

"Don't be confused by Violet," Jack replied. "She's far more experienced than her powder and lipstick would indicate."

Violet squeezed his hand threateningly. "All of you loved her?" she asked Mr. Tanner.

"To varying degrees. You have to understand, photographs and paintings don't do Rachael justice. She had a way of looking at you, this softness and sweetness that never can be captured by a photograph. It was ensnaring. She was merry too. Ready to laugh. It wasn't only me. She inexplicably loved me over them, but we all loved her."

Violet wasn't sure that would have been true in other circumstances. There were other females at the university, but this one was something of a captive bird. Perhaps they all fancied themselves as knights and rescuers even if it didn't sound as though she were trying to escape.

Maybe they each fancied himself as her next keeper? They'd 'rescue' her from her uncle and then protect her themselves? Violet imagined that the idea could appeal to a romantic but very young heart.

"How did Mr. Allen get the photograph from you?"

Mr. Tanner glanced at Violet. "You weren't the only one who realized what I'd done. I don't work for Professor Morgan anymore. I avoid his lectures. I avoid him at all costs if I can. I needed to see her face. I couldn't go the rest of my life and forget the shape of her smile. I had notes from her to cling to, but I needed her face. I...just needed it."

"So he asked you for it?" Violet asked gently. "He saw you take it too? And he found you?"

"I walk a lot at night now. He knew that. He'd followed me too many times, trying to find out what I was up to. He challenged me for it. Told me he'd tell Morgan what I'd done if I didn't give it to him. I..." Tanner sighed. "I was going to take it back later. It wasn't worth the argument."

"Who did she encourage?" Jack asked. "Did he want the photograph because he loved her?"

Violet answered for him. "If she was giving someone else hope, she wasn't doing it while he was around."

Mr. Tanner flushed furiously, and Violet felt certain that the transition between pale and red as grief and anger hit him in waves was going to have him fainting like his sweet Miss Morgan. Violet rose to pace.

"Was this Elijah rich?" Violet asked. "The one who Mr. Morgan wanted her to wed?"

"Ah, well, yes," Mr. Tanner answered.

"You hesitated." Violet turned and pursed her mouth as she thought. "Was he rich by your standards? Or was he rich by the non-scholarship student standards?"

Mr. Tanner had to think about that for a few minutes. "Elijah needed to have a career. His expected income from his family wouldn't have been enough to support him without working."

"That's the way it is for most these days." Jack watched Violet, who nodded.

"There can only be so many rich great aunts," Violet said sarcastically and continued to pace, moving on to fiddling with her ring. She glanced down at it and wondered if Jack had a ring in his pocket. Did he get into the water with the ring? Did it have river water and dead body fluid on it now? She shivered but knew she'd clean it well and wear it happily. Knowing Jack, however, he had already cleaned it should it have gotten wet.

Her gaze lit on him, and her heart lit with love. There was a man who would have noticed if she was being slowly killed and would have saved her. Not that she blamed anyone who hadn't seen the slow death of Miss Morgan. Violet felt certain that there was every reason to believe her heart was failing her and not that she was being murdered.

"How did Mr. Allen know?" Violet asked Jack. "What made him think it when no one else did?"

"I think it might have been a wild guess," Jack replied. "When he was a boy, he saw a crime in every movement. He was like Ham is—prone to see a pickpocket in every bumped shoulder, a murder in every dead body, a grand scheme in every passed note. He was still young. He might not have grown out of that yet."

"He hadn't," Mr. Tanner replied. "He believed that one of the students in our class had stolen the test questions. He believed that one of the religion students was running a brothel. He...his ideas were wild, and he was a joke."

Violet winced for the boy and realized he must have been a laughingstock. "He used his father's money to propel him. He must have had quite an excess to get people who had money themselves to take note."

"He paid for everything, all the time." Tanner shook his head. "He'd order cases of things to an excess. I haven't bought myself cigarettes since he started hanging about. He would just fill up your cigarette case. He was recklessly generous. He told me once that someone was taking the cash from his rooms, and that was the only crime I ever believed. He'd leave it in a bowl on his desk. He never even changed his habits after he said that. He kept leaving it in a bowl on his desk and tried to catch the fellow."

"He never did?" Violet asked.

"I don't think it was only one person," Tanner admitted. "I think it was a few of them, and he ruled out people I wouldn't have ruled out. He ruled out everyone who was very wealthy, but I think the lads who were doing it did so to watch him scurry around, not to take the money. At least the ones who kept taking it."

"That poor fool," Violet murmured. She glanced at Jack, who looked pained for the lad. He had cared about Jeremy once. He had never stopped, Violet thought, and this must be killing him. "He stumbled onto a real crime in a sea of shadows."

Jack cursed, revealing just how much he was affected. Was he seeing the boy he'd once known? Violet bet that it was awfully like how she felt about Ginny. Violet's Ginny—Vi would throw herself into the lion's den for the girl.

"Jack..." Her sympathy was evident in her tone, and he turned to her, letting her see the pain in his gaze. They both glanced at Tanner, but he was drowning in his own pain. Violet crossed to Jack, looking down on him where he sat. His shoulders were as tense as Rodin's Thinker. Violet took hold of his shoulder. He was not alone. He wasn't going to be alone again.

"I didn't think it could be right," Jack muttered low. "I thought, like Tanner, I thought Jeremy was on another one of his pirate treasure hunts like when he was a boy."

"It's not our fault, Jack," she said quietly, but Tanner looked up at the comment. "It's not Tanner's fault he thought Jeremy was wrong. It's not my fault that I didn't give into Miss Allen's black-mail. It's not—"

"Blackmail?" Jack's cold tone made Violet flinch.

She hesitated, but Jack's expression made it clear that he wasn't going to accept anything less than a full story. "We were right about her guesses with V.V. Twinnings. She felt that the knowledge would be sufficient for me to bend to her will. And then bend you to her will."

Jack's eyes narrowed and the muscle in his jaw clenched repet-itively. "How?"

"She wanted you to fix things as much as possible with her brother's professors. I suppose, looking back, she realized he was on one of his random investigations. She wanted you to step in and straighten him out."

"Why would I do that for you and not simply because I care about Jeremy?"

"Because," Violet said, inwardly wincing to have to repeat it, "you would do anything for the woman you love. She said no one knew that better than her."

CHAPTER SIXTEEN

*J*ack took Tanner with him to find Hamilton. He placed the journal in Violet's hands and asked her to read it for him. Something Jeremiah Allen had stumbled across was something worth killing over. With any luck, Violet would recognize what was real in the sea of nonsense.

It suddenly made sense to Violet why Miss Allen had handed the journal over. She had no idea which of her brother's wild theories caused his death and which were paranoid fantasies.

Violet cleared her throat and took a long breath in as she opened the journal. She blinked rapidly and then stared. Mr. Allen had written in multiple languages. It might even be in code. She realized it was an excellent thing that her twin had fallen in love with a woman who was far cleverer than Violet. Especially when it came to things like languages and codes.

Violet went to the bedroom where Beatrice had gone with the dogs. She found the maid mending stockings with both spaniels at her feet.

"My lady?"

Violet smiled at her and asked, "Did you get some tea?"

The maid shook her head, but her expression was hesitant. "I made a mistake, my lady."

"Just throw the stockings out, dear. Don't worry."

"No, I mean...the stockings are fine. But I...when I was packing your things at Mr. Morgan's house, I added the writing chest to your case. I should have realized I didn't pack it for you when you left."

"Don't worry, love. We'll send it back with Jack and our apologies."

Beatrice nodded but acted as though there was more to it. "My lady...I dropped it. And there was a hidden compartment."

Violet's eyes widened as curiosity hit her. Now Beatrice's worry made sense.

"What secrets did you find? Shall we have to send a whole case of liquid apologies? This is why we keep Victor around, you know."

"There are love letters," Beatrice said. "I didn't mean to see them. But I was afraid...I mean..."

"You wanted to know how badly your mistake might be."

The maid nodded. "I thought you would be very upset."

Violet winked. "Don't worry, love. I would be lost without you."

When Violet returned to the combination sitting and dining room, Victor and Kate had come back. She set the letters from the writing chest down on the table and looked at her brother.

"We got Tanner a room," Victor said. "But it seems we've lost him."

"Jack took him to find Hamilton. I think Jack believes him, but he won't be leaving any of the suspects here with us."

"With you," Kate said, smiling.

Violet shrugged and then tossed the journal to Kate. "I have a job for you, darling. Mr. Allen's journal is written in multiple languages, and Jack has entrusted us with discovering what we can."

Kate took it, grinning. "What fun."

Violet recapped what they'd learned from Mr. Tanner before Kate retreated to dig through what she could of the journal. While Violet had been speaking, Lila and Ginny had returned and Denny had awoken from his nap.

"Do the thing," Denny told her. "With the journal and the list."

She showed them the love letters first, and Denny rubbed his hands together and picked up one. He cleared his throat before reading.

R,

Seeing you today and being unable to take you into my arms was more painful than torture. Your eyes...

Denny looked up. "It's just full of praise and compliments. Lila darling, shall I plagiarize this for you?"

"I'll pass," Lila said dryly, "but it seems young Ginny is intrigued."

Ginny leaned forward and tugged the letter from Denny's hand. She glanced it over. "Who is E? Is that the one that went off with Jack? Do you think that he will mourn her endlessly? Like Romeo would if he'd lived?"

Violet glanced at Victor, who shuddered at Ginny's reference to Romeo and Juliet. "What is it with these ladies and that bedamned tale? Ginny, would you truly want the man you loved to kill himself if you died?"

Ginny considered and then admitted, "It is romantic."

"That's all it is, my dear. As we have discussed before, Victor, Romeo and Juliet is not a real story and real children did not die."

"Well, if they had lived, they were too stupid to carry on," he muttered.

Violet snorted and smacked her brother on the shoulder.

"What about you, Violet? Would you want Jack to love again if you died?" Ginny's gaze was fixed on Violet, who nodded immediately.

"I would want Jack to enjoy every second of his life. That's part of loving, Ginny darling." Violet paused a moment and then asked, "Did you say E? An E signed the letter?"

Denny nodded.

"Are you sure it isn't an N?"

Denny showed Violet the letter, then she flipped through the whole stack. There were two sets of handwriting. No...there was a third as well. The last was feminine, and Violet guessed that it was Rachael herself.

Ginny was watching. "She had two lovers? That's far less romantic."

Violet opened Rachael's last letter. It started, 'My dearest Nathan.' He must have been the one she truly loved. Had she been playing the two against each other? Or had she been trying to keep one at bay while she waited for the other to propose?

"I am not so sympathetic for her now," Ginny told Violet and Victor.

"She was ill, Ginny darling," Vi told her. "She was dependent on her uncle, who had chosen one man for her while she loved another. She was killed for some reason...maybe because she loved the wrong man? Maybe because of these letters? Maybe for another reason we don't yet know, but I can assure you that losing her life is punishment enough."

Ginny frowned. "How did she die?"

"Someone she believed she could trust poisoned her," Violet told her.

"Maybe we should blunt it a little for her, Violet." Victor's gaze was fixed on the expression on their young ward.

"Victor, Ginny has been through quite a lot already. She isn't your average spoiled child."

"I know but..." He glanced at Violet and then at Kate. "I'd love for her to be."

"Which is why we all adore you," Kate told him, running her hand over Ginny's back.

"If we want her to be mature," Violet told Victor, "and accept that the spoiled brats at her school are not worth ruining her life over, then we need to treat her as the nearly grownup young woman she is."

Victor scowled. "You're going to do better in your classes then?" he asked the young woman in question.

Ginny nodded, jaw firming.

"Who do you think killed her?" Denny asked, bringing them back to the matter at hand. "Someone send for a chalkboard. Let's do the thing."

Violet nodded at Beatrice, who had been waiting nearby, and the girl stepped out of the hotel suite.

"Who do you think killed her?" Kate repeated.

Violet shrugged, uncertain. "Is there anything in the journal?"

Kate flipped through the pages. "There's no pattern to it."

Violet glanced at everyone, who was looking at her for answers. She hated investigations like this one. The ones where the crime was so terrible. When Mr. Danvers had been killed, Violet's predominant emotion had been relief for Isolde. When Bettina Marino had been killed, Violet had felt regret for the woman, but she'd hardly been innocent.

Rachael Morgan, however, had been killed despite not doing anything to deserve it. Violet was well aware that no one truly deserved to be murdered, but sometimes the crime felt far more wicked. She paced as she thought and every time she looked up, she found Denny's gaze on her, his mouth twitching.

"Stop it," she told him.

"It looks like hard work," he said. "Someone call for more cold drinks. Lila, love?"

"You have hands and a mouth, darling."

"But you always remember the other things that go so nicely with drinks."

Lila rose, a long-suffering look on her face, and turned to Ginny. "This, darling, is what real love looks like. Somehow wanting to be with someone despite all their odd little foibles."

Lila made the order as Beatrice came back with several of the hotel porters, who rolled in a chalkboard. Beatrice was carrying a box full of chalk that she handed to Violet. Vi took a piece of chalk from the box, placed the rest on one of the tables and paced in front of the blank chalkboard.

"Was there nothing in the journal?"

Kate shook her head. "It's all nonsense."

"Then we need to start with Rachael Morgan and see if we can find an overlap between what we know of her and what that journal has in it."

Violet wrote on the chalkboard.

RACHAEL MORGAN —

It took Vi a long time to think about what she knew of Rachael Morgan. Some of it had to be incidental, and some of it was relevant.

"She was an heiress," Ginny said. "That mattered when it was your aunt."

Violet nodded and added it after Rachael's name. Then she followed it up with: Who was her heir? Mr. Morgan? Another relative we haven't met?

"She was beloved of that E fellow and Mr. Tanner," Ginny

added again. "Mr. Danvers was killed because his son loved Isolde."

Violet glanced at the girl, who was staring just as seriously at the board as Violet. It was a little intoxicating, Violet thought, noting the way Ginny's head tilted like Kate's did. The way she glanced at Violet and then back at the board, searching for something to contribute. Ginny's desire to be like them—to be included—it must have been similar between Jack and poor Mr. Allen.

Violet added: Rachael had two lovers.

"People kill over love," Ginny said. "I don't understand it."

"But you think it's romantic that Romeo and Juliet killed themselves?" If Victor's tone had been mocking, Violet would have had to hit him fiercely over the head.

"Well..." Ginny considered. "They made that choice. It wasn't someone killing the person they loved because they couldn't have them. That doesn't feel very much like love."

"It's not," Violet agreed. "But we only have the words on the letters. We don't know if the feeling behind the words was real. She was lovely, and for these boys, she was as well-connected as you could wish. She was valuable to them. Like a commodity."

Ginny gasped, her eyes glinting, and Violet nodded. Exactly that reaction—that was the one that Violet wanted to encourage in Ginny. The utter rejection of herself as something to be bargained with.

Violet turned back to the chalkboard and wrote: Treated as a commodity. Whether Violet felt it was right or fair, the truth was the girl *had* an inheritance and her uncle had hoped she'd love one of his lads. Had there been some bargaining between her uncle and this E? Perhaps. Perhaps the uncle had tried to manipulate events and bargain with Miss Morgan's inheritance.

Violet wrote 'money' after Rachael's name as well. She frowned as she examined the board. She added, 'weak heart.'

Violet read the board aloud when she was done.

RACHAEL MORGAN — Heiress. Who was her heir? Mr. Morgan? Another relative we haven't met? Rachael had two lovers. E (Elijah) and Mr. Nathan Tanner. Treated as a commodity. The money? Or just the connection? Weak heart.

Violet tilted her head as she examined the list. "I am not a physician. However, I wonder how much this—" Violet underlined weak heart, "—came into play with the murder. Whoever killed Rachael Morgan knew to take advantage of that."

"What are you saying?" Victor had followed her thought process, and the twins turned to each other. "That they were putting her down like a horse with a broken leg?"

Violet's mouth twisted at the thought. "I don't like the idea any more than you do."

"Someone who kills a poor innocent girl," Lila clarified, "might have thought like that. We aren't talking about someone who reasons normally."

"Poisoning this girl and watching her slowly fade away—that's not a crime of passion that one of us could understand even if we would never commit an act like that. Rachael Morgan's murder was an act of cold-blooded cruelty. They poisoned her and continued to interact with her while she died, patiently waiting without ever being moved to enough compassion to save her."

"That's horrifying," Ginny said, wiping away a tear.

Violet crossed to the girl, hugging her tight and glancing around the room. Lila and Denny both had fierce frowns. Victor and Kate were holding hands, their fingers gripping so hard that Violet could see the impressions of their digits digging in.

"Murders are horrifying by their nature."

"Why do you get involved?" Ginny asked suddenly.

"Jack feels guilty for what happened to Mr. Allen, Ginny. As do I, to an extent. If I can help alleviate that guilt, if I can help find Rachael Morgan justice, it's worth some of the horror."

Ginny nodded, angrily wiping away her tear. "Will you have nightmares later?"

Violet nodded.

"I will too."

"We all will," Victor told Ginny. She glanced at him, looking for a lie and finding only truth. She shivered once and curled into Violet's side.

CHAPTER SEVENTEEN

*B*eatrice was setting up the dinner table when there was a knock on the door. Violet nodded to the chalkboard, and Denny and Victor swiftly turned it to face the wall. Once their notes were hidden, Victor opened the door.

They'd paused on their list of suspects while Violet glanced through the journal herself. Kate was right, it was a mess that would take weeks and weeks to translate and sort out. Violet had sighed. "What about the love letters?"

Denny had answered. "They're all from E and Nate. The ones from Nate are more specific. Like that relationship was more real."

"That matches up with Mr. Tanner's story."

Violet glanced to the door and saw that he had returned with both Jack and Hamilton.

"Just in time to join us for dinner," Violet said. "Did you learn anything?"

Jack smiled at her, but he didn't answer other than to press a kiss on her cheek.

"The food will be here soon," she told him. "Let's dress for dinner and then compare notes."

The chance to freshen up was a welcome one. Jack, Hamilton, and Mr. Tanner had already dressed, so the women left them making cocktails while they escaped to their bedrooms.

Violet winked at Jack and stepped into her bedroom, closing the door. Her dress was already hanging on the mirror, and Violet removed her day dress, exchanging her nude stockings for black ones. She dropped the red-beaded dress over her head, fluffed her hair, brightened her lipstick, and then added a strand of black pearls.

It took only minutes for Violet to change and when she returned to the combined dining and sitting room in their suite, Jack, Hamilton, and Mr. Tanner had turned Violet's chalkboard around and were reading it. She had only gone so far as to add additional names but hadn't filled in any of the details.

The names were:

MR. MORGAN

MR. NATHAN TANNER

MR. ELIJAH _____

THE OTHER MAN WITH ELIJAH AT THE RECEPTION

MISS MORGAN'S HEIR

PROFESSOR SNAG

"Me?" Mr. Tanner demanded. "Why me? I loved her."

"But did she love you?" Violet asked him gently.

"Of course she did," Mr. Tanner stuttered, and Violet glanced to Jack and Hamilton, who were examining the comments following Miss Morgan's name.

"She's got the pertinent details," Hamilton told Jack. "Did you do this by yourself?"

Lila answered for Violet. "She's the only one who would. No

offense, Mr. Tanner, but the rest of us aren't emotionally involved and there's a reason we have gents like Jack."

"I might have figured it out," Victor said. "Though my hand-writing would have been much sloppier. Kate could have done it as well. Not all of us are as infernally lazy as you and Denny."

Lila's expression told Violet just what she thought of that comment.

"Morgan?" Jack asked Violet.

"He has to be a suspect."

"But why?" Jack demanded. "He's rich. He loved her. I know he did. He worried over her constantly."

"You don't know the internal workings of his heart, Jack. He was close to her. He could have easily been her heir. She wasn't doing as he wished. A scholarship student? When there was that Elijah fellow? She had a secret love."

"Morgan has money of his own, and people have dealt with their children doing other than they wished for centuries without killing them." Jack sighed. "He's my friend, Violet."

"My cousin killed my aunt, Jack. People aren't always what we want them to be. Besides, he's just on the list. I vote for this Elijah fellow. He was there last night, he had to have been irri-tated by Jeremiah, he supposedly loved Rachael, and she loved another."

Jack nodded with a frown. "All right then."

There was another knock on the door, and Beatrice let in the porters with the dinner. She and Mr. Giles served the food, but Violet avoided eating to stare at the list of suspects. Finally, with dinner mostly gone, she rose and picked up her chalk.

"What is this Elijah fellow's last name?" Violet asked.

"Ballard," Mr. Tanner said.

"Sir Ferdinand Ballard's son?"

Mr. Tanner nodded. "One of the younger ones I believe."

"He really won't have an inheritance," Victor said. "Even the oldest son doesn't have much coming his way. Don't they have a good half-dozen sons, Vi?"

She nodded and added, "Along with several daughters. Miss Morgan and her money must have been quite appealing to Elijah."

"She was far more than her money," Mr. Tanner snapped.

"I'm sure she was," Violet told him. "To you at least."

"Am I off the suspect list yet?"

Violet shook her head and grinned merrily at him.

"Not if Morgan isn't," Jack said.

"Don't worry, Mr. Tanner, I haven't put up Miss Allen or her father yet."

"Why would Miss Allen kill Rachael?" Mr. Tanner asked.

Jack turned to Violet and waited. If he was offended or in agreement, she couldn't tell. Her gaze was not nearly as all-knowing and penetrating as his. She grinned at him and said, "I don't think she did. But, if she killed Jeremiah Allen, then..."

"Then our guess about Miss Morgan dying was wrong, and she's playing games with all of us."

"Jeremiah might need his own chalkboard if we take that approach," Jack said. "Was there anything to be found in the journal?"

"No," Violet said. "Not yet anyway. Kate is working on it, but young Mr. Allen was paranoid."

"He was living some sort of fantasy like one of the Allan Quatermain books when he was a boy," Jack said.

"Or maybe the habit extended to his adulthood and nothing more," Hamilton said gently. "He wasn't the boy you knew, Jack. He was an adult. He used skills he learned as a boy to keep his notes. You aren't avenging that boy, you are avenging the man he became."

Jack nodded. "I suppose I feel guilty because I left him."

"Emily cheated on you with a friend from our regiment, Jack. You found them in bed together, and you made the right choice. You weren't Jeremiah's father—he had one. One who bought his son's way into this mess."

Victor choked on Hamilton's revelation, but Violet knew it was meant for her. She added, "She wants you back."

Jack's expression was mocking. "With you or without you, Violet Carlyle, that will never happen."

She kept her expression even and nodded at him once. He had told her she didn't need to be jealous, and she had believed him. She felt it to her bones now. She crossed to the chalkboard and faced the others. "Who was Miss Morgan's heir?"

"Daniel," Jack said with a sigh. "He has his own money, Violet."

She nodded, but she filled in the information on her chalkboard.

MR. MORGAN — Miss Morgan's heir. Was her death the result of greed?

MR. NATHAN TANNER — He said he loved Miss Morgan, but she was writing notes with two men. Did he decide that if he couldn't have her, no one could?

MR. ELIJAH BALLARD —Mr. Morgan's intended for Rachael. Did he know that the woman he expected to marry loved another? Did he decide that if he couldn't have her, no one could?

PROFESSOR SNAG— Jeremiah Allen searched his office. Why? Something about the murder or some other supposed crime?

"Did anyone have alibis?" Violet asked.

Mr. Tanner sighed and then said, "Professor Snag was ill."

"Jack," Violet said, turning to him. "Is Jeremiah's father here?"

Jack nodded. "I need to see if he knew anything, don't I? He's staying here with his daughter." Jack pointedly did not say Miss Allen's name.

"Into the lioness's den, laddie," Lila told him. "Keep an eye on your virtue."

He stood, adjusting his jacket, and then he left. Violet turned back to the chalkboard, refusing to be concerned.

"It's a good thing Jack's such a good man," Victor said to remind Violet. "Otherwise, one might have to worry about that viper, Emily Allen."

Violet didn't reply, but Kate did. "And yet there is no reason for any of us to worry since he is a good man."

Ginny had been sent down to her tutor's room for the evening, and the rest of them examined the chalkboard as they considered.

"I want to talk to Elijah." Violet glanced at Mr. Tanner. "You could get him to come here."

"Why would he?" Mr. Tanner asked.

"Tell him of a research opportunity with *the* Hamilton Barnes. Say that he has to report this evening and be of good assistance, and he is guaranteed to..."

Violet turned to Hamilton, who shrugged. "Ah...perhaps, the chance to shadow some of our best investigators. Something to... write a journal article about? Or..."

"And also," Violet added, "the chance to write it up in a newspaper. We'll get the Piccadilly Press to publish it."

"How?" Victor demanded.

"Do you think the young Mr. Allen is the only one who bought his life? I bet Mr. Allen bought Miss Allen's position at that paper. Also—" Vi hesitated, "...so we can't necessarily arrange it. We can try to arrange it somewhere else if that doesn't work or apologize and offer a consolation prize." Violet looked at Mr. Tanner, who rose and crossed to the telephone.

While he made the phone call, Violet had Beatrice clear the room.

"Should we hide the chalkboard?" Victor asked.

Violet shook her head. "Why not let him see what we're thinking?"

"Maybe we should invite Morgan as well," Hamilton suggested. "While Jack is gone and can't object."

"Who do you think killed them?"

Hamilton's head bowed, and he sighed.

"You know what we should do," Denny said. "Actually..." He dropped to his knees, folding his fingers together and begged. "That Elijah bloke, Morgan, that other guy—I wasn't really paying attention—that wench Emily. All of them. Gather them up. Peel away their secrets. Throw them out for your—our—well, my enjoyment, and you and Jack do your thing."

"What?" Violet demanded.

Hamilton brightened. "It could work. I don't like to see Jack suffering. He's suffering over that boy, his sister, you being here and seeing this part of his life. I'll call Morgan."

Violet glanced at Lila, whose mouth was twitching. "Please don't make me leave."

"We're not leaving," Victor told Kate, Lila, and Denny. "We're part of this."

"You aren't part of it," Violet told him.

"Neither are you," Victor countered.

She smiled at him, and they turned as one to Hamilton. "You'll need us," she told him. "We put pressure on, but we also make it seem innocent. 'We're worried about Jack, Morgan. Come to the hotel. Have a drink with him and that girl he loves. The spoiled earl's daughter and her brother.'"

He agreed. "I'll call down to speak to Jack and have him invite those two Allens up."

"We need it to look innocent in here. Beatrice, bring desserts. Order a bunch of the flashy stuff. Whatever you can get. Make it look festive. Like a bright young thing party, as if we're a few minutes from putting on a fancy dress and running drunken through the streets."

Hamilton snorted, and Violet winked at him. "We're just a few months from getting you to join us on one of those treasure hunts, my friend."

Hamilton rose and connected to the Allens' suite. Violet could hear Ham's side of the conversation. "Jack. We're calling up all the suspects. We're going to try to pin one down and end things."

Jack's voice was a rumble on other side of the telephone, but considering he had an audience, it must have been coded for Hamilton.

"I know it's unusual and probably unprofessional, but this whole case is a mess, Jack. These are our friends. The boy who died was the younger brother of your former fiancé. It needs to be unequivocal."

Hamilton finished the telephone call and turned, nodding to Violet.

"Play it dramatic," Violet told Tanner. "And don't destroy my faith in you and be the killer."

"I'm not," Tanner told Violet, but she didn't say anything. She wasn't going to pretend to have faith in him. She didn't have that.

"Make the chalkboard indecent, Violet," Hamilton said. "Use your friends and their wit. Make it look as bad as you can. Kate, I understand you're quite good at languages?"

She nodded.

"Pretend Jeremiah's journal supports everything you can put on the board. Use as much as we believe, but make it worse."

Kate nodded again.

"Whoever killed that boy tracked him through a quiet town,

beat him pretty well, knocked him out, and threw him in the river alive, where he drowned before he could save himself."

Violet gasped, biting her lip.

"The rest of them know pieces of it," Hamilton said. "I don't care what it takes to get those pieces out. The man who saved my life more times than I can count and who has never once cared that I am a miller's son from the back of beyond loved that boy. We're catching the killer for Jack."

Violet nodded, gritting her teeth as she approached the chalkboard.

"For Jack," Victor repeated.

"For Jack," Denny said. "Plus it'll be fun to make the killer squirm."

"Oh, my lad," Lila said, "don't make a joke of it."

"If I don't, I might sick up, my love."

CHAPTER EIGHTEEN

They had taken the largest suite the hotel had, but it was still crowded. Even with the table loaded with cakes and sweets tucked back by the wall, more chairs had been brought for those who came to be interrogated, and with the chalkboard taking up the last of the space, there was very little room left.

Violet and Victor turned the chalkboard back around and placed a covering on it that could be pulled down. Kate pulled random things from Allen's journal as the twins wove them into fictions they added to the names on the board, mixing in the truth whenever possible but changing the angle of the truths to make it seem all the more terrible.

"I think everything else is ready to go, my lady," Beatrice told Violet.

"Wonderful," Violet answered without looking away from where she wrote, 'Did Morgan have unnatural feelings for his niece? Was that why she died? If he couldn't have her, no one could?' "You may have the evening off. Be safe, love."

Victor was being particularly vicious under Miss Allen's heading, with comments about the inheritance and her relationship with Jeremiah.

"He did say to be salacious," Victor told Violet when she winced at one of the things he wrote.

"You've got that down, my brother," Denny told Victor as he came to read the board. He chuckled evilly. "You have a future in truly offensive fiction." He chuckled again and called to Lila, "Can you imagine, beloved? If they wrote truly lewd fiction? Their stepmother? I shudder in fear for them, but the show, my beloved, the show! Say we can attend when the day arrives? Please?"

Violet glanced at her brother. They were being horrible human beings. She was ashamed of them. Aunt Agatha would be ashamed, Vi thought. This wasn't just finding the killer, it was torturing the other mourners.

"For Jack," Victor said to her, ignoring Denny's giggling.

"I'm not sure Jack would approve of this."

"He doesn't," Jack said, placing a hand on her hip as he leaned around her to read the chalkboard. "Emily and her father will be here soon."

"I'm sorry," Violet told him, hating this situation.

"You want to go to the sea, don't you? We'll wrap this up and go somewhere cooler than London in the middle of summer."

Violet grinned, but it faded immediately as he read the chalkboard. His gaze moved over the comments under each of the names. Then, with a wink, Jack added his own terrible details using things only he could know. "Jeremiah would have loved this. It makes this farce easier. Even this stuff about Emily—he loved his sister—but he'd have let her squirm."

"Tanner, leave," Jack ordered without moving from the board. "Come back in a half an hour. Make that thirty-five minutes. Be late. Show up as though you didn't know what was happening. Act like the rest of them."

"I'll do whatever you want, but I need a picture of Rachael when this is over. I don't want to forget her face."

"Feed the situation and I'll see you get one."

Victor had just set down his chalk and wiped his hands when Jack finished. Victor tossed the cloth he'd used to Jack, looking at the board. "That might be the most horrific piece of fiction we have ever written, and we wrote about a man masquerading as a ghost in order to make an innocent young woman fall in love with him. Only then he let her suffer while he verified her love."

"It's your intentions that matter," Kate told him as Victor muttered, frowning at the chalkboard.

"My love," Victor said, "some of these will hurt. The Scarlet Ghost was as fictional as your Romeo and Juliet."

"Sadly," Kate said, reaching out and taking his hand, "Jeremiah Allen and Rachael Morgan are not fictional."

"If it helps," Denny said lazily, "this is my favorite fiction yet. It makes my friend, the Scarlet Ghost, seem trite."

"You know what it makes," Jack said carefully. "It makes Romeo and Juliet and their willingness to kill themselves for love seem romantic. Better that than these unnatural feelings between uncle and niece."

"That part was Violet," Victor said with a snort, shaking off the morose mood. "You should remember that about her."

There was a knock at the door, and Jack said, "Let the play begin."

Victor swiftly flipped down the covering over the chalkboard.

Mr. Allen and his daughter were the first to arrive. He was not nearly as comely as his daughter. His eyes, however, were brilliant. Sharp and clever. They were surrounded, however, by a pockmarked faced, an oversized red nose, and thick, chapped lips.

Mr. Allen took in the covered chalkboard, the cocktail Victor handed him, and Hamilton and Jack. "Playing games, lads? I'd be furious if I didn't know you were hunting my boy's killer."

Jack didn't confirm, but Miss Allen looked from her father back to Jack and then walked over to lift the chalkboard cover, reading what was underneath it.

"My feelings will be quite hurt, Jack darling, if Father is wrong about the purpose of this charade. This is not nice."

"Play along, Emily. Don't mess things up with Jack again." Mr. Allen's voice boomed, making Violet flinch.

Violet glanced at Jack, who shook his head slightly. She nibbled her bottom lip to keep from lashing out at Emily. It wasn't that Violet didn't trust Jack, but the assumption that things were corrected between Jack and Emily infuriated Violet. Before Emily and her father could break into a real argument, Mr. Morgan arrived. He shook hands heartily and crossed to Hamilton to speak of the case. Violet watched him move through the room completely at ease.

Was it normal to treat this investigation as a dinner party? Of course, they'd invited him as though they were having a bit of a cocktail party. Except when you arrived to that event, surely you would at least muster up the pretense of sorrow when the dead person's family was present?

Violet frowned as she watched him, and then young Elijah Ballard appeared. His eyes were wide and shocked as he realized that the Allens were in attendance. He glanced around, taking in the set-up and frowning. It was clear that all was amiss, and he swallowed.

Professor Snag was the next to arrive, followed by two of Mr. Morgan's assistants.

"I didn't know the boys would be here, Jack," Mr. Morgan said. "What's going on?"

"This is all Ham, my friend," Jack said. His expression was smooth but stiff.

"What's all this about, Ham?" Snag asked as Nathan Tanner appeared next. "Nathan, my boy."

Hamilton stood, presenting himself rather like he had at the lecture. "My friends, lads, Emily, thank you for coming. Please help yourself to cocktails and pudding. Perhaps a few comforts will make what happens next all the easier."

"What's this all about, Ham?" Morgan's voice rose. "What the devil, my good man, is happening here?"

What the devil indeed, Violet thought. Why was he jumping to anger so quickly? Violet glanced at Jack, whose gaze was fixed on his friend.

Hamilton ignored Morgan's outburst and said idly, "Well, have it your way instead of having the sweets, Daniel. You're all here because you're under suspicion of murder. A double murder actually."

Mr. Morgan's choked and started to stand, but Hamilton snapped, "You *will* sit down."

Hamilton paused while the others settled back down. Once the objections stopped, Morgan spoke again, voice carrying, "We don't have to put up with this, Hamilton."

"You don't," Hamilton replied. "You can leave here, and we can give our evidence to the local boys, who will arrest you on suspicion of murder. We have rather enough reason for all of you to be questioned further. I wonder what the dean will think of that, Daniel? You know he and I are rather good friends. Shall I call him and invite him to our little tête-a-tête? Explain to him how you won't answer a few questions about the murder of one of the students and your own niece?"

"Niece?" Morgan flushed, and his large eyebrows turned down, accentuating his fierce frown so much it seemed impossible that anyone could be as angry as this man at this time. He waved his hand, seeming to give Hamilton permission to proceed, but his voice was very clear as he said, "You are not the only one with friends in high places, Hamilton."

Violet glanced at Ham, who had flushed. That must, she thought, be a real threat for Hamilton.

She could give him a career. Easily. But it wouldn't be what he'd worked the entirety of his life for. She had a ridiculous amount of money but saving him if this all went south might be out of even her reach.

Her head tilted as she examined him, and he smiled at her. He knew she was worried for him, and his eyes glinted with understanding. The two of them stared at each other and then Violet nodded. *For Jack, who carried guilt.* For Jeremiah, taken too early. For all of them who needed to escape this madness. Even for Emily, who loved her brother. For all of them except the killer.

CHAPTER NINETEEN

*H*amilton slowly uncovered the chalkboard. The room was silent as the gathered suspects read. Then shouts of anger filled the space, and the younger lads looked at each other and back at the board, eyes wide and fixed. They seemed ready to run, but Mr. Barnes's threat kept them quiet and in their seats.

Mr. Tanner, however, did not watch Barnes like the rest. He didn't read the board. He watched everyone else in the room react, and his mouth twitched. He was happy, Violet guessed.

"What is this about me?" Professor Snag demanded. He had a bushy mustache and bald head, and rather kind eyes. "Why am I on this board, Barnes? What's this about Miss Morgan having been killed? My man, she had a weak heart. You've known it since she was a child. Her heart failed her. There's no reason to believe she was murdered."

"She was poisoned," Hamilton replied calmly. "Why do you think Jeremiah Allen was so excitable about decomposing flesh? He dug her up and had someone look for evidence."

"What?" Mr. Morgan's enraged shout had them all turning his way. "What is this nonsense? Unnatural love? Her money? Why would I kill my niece for her money? How could you believe that? How could you believe any of this?"

"The money became solely hers the moment she married," Nathan Tanner said quietly. "Elijah talked about it often. Her allowance, he was obsessed with it. There was a ticking time clock on when that money stopped being Mr. Morgan's to access."

Elijah turned on Nathan Tanner, gaze narrowed on him. "I? I talked about it often? You were obsessed with her, scholarship boy. Do you think we don't know it was her money that called to you?"

"They've turned on each other so quickly," Denny whispered to Violet as they stood at the back of the room with the others. He rubbed his hand together in near glee.

"How long would it take you to turn on us?" Victor asked Denny, lifting a brow.

Denny winked. "Turning on you would be too much trouble."

"He's too lazy for that," Lila added quietly, "and my truest love is Violet, so he wouldn't have me around looking after him."

Violet smiled at Lila and arched a brow at Denny, who nodded and whispered, "It's true. She loves Vi the most."

The shouting had finally quieted enough for Hamilton to explain. "We are looking to refute these claims, gents. Calm down. Perhaps you would like to go first, Snag. You asked why you were here. There are some claims about you. Tell us why they aren't true."

"It's simple enough for me, Barnes. I didn't have a reason to kill Miss Morgan. I had no chance at her money. I was not her lover. I was a friend of her uncle who saw her on occasion and never missed her when I didn't see her."

"And young Allen?" Hamilton asked.

"I wasn't even in Oxford yesterday. It was the reason why I sent Tanner to your reception. I did not kill the girl or Allen. Tanner would not have killed the girl. Anyone who knew him while she was alive knew he adored her. He'd have laid down in a puddle and let her walk over his back to keep her feet dry."

Hamilton glanced at Morgan, whose face was furiously red.

"Why do you know that?" Jack asked Professor Snag.

He shrugged, glancing Morgan, "Sorry old boy," Snag started. "I'm a bit of a romantic. Rachael loved Nathan. Nathan loved Rachael. I...helped when I could."

"He is a scholarship student with no family," Morgan shouted. "Why would you think that he was good enough for my girl?"

"Rachael had options, Daniel. She chose. It was as simple as that. You can't control a girl's heart."

Violet bit her bottom lip to keep from shouting a 'Hallelujah.'

Lila, however, muttered, "Hear, hear."

Denny reached out and put his hand over his wife's mouth. "Hush, love. They'll kick us out. This is my favorite part."

Jack was the only one to turn their way, but Lila winked at him with Denny's hand still over her mouth. His eyes glinted with a flash of humor, and he shook his head at Hamilton. Violet elbowed Denny, who mimed buttoning his mouth.

Hamilton ignored all of them. "Snag, we'll check out your stories. Did you have anything to add?"

Snag read over the chalkboard and opened his mouth to speak. Hamilton shot him a look, intent upon his next words, but Snag said, "I think I'll save my comments for later. But I do think you can remove young Marcus from the list. He was not in love with Rachael. And though we all found the younger Mr. Allen irritating, Marcus had no reason to kill the boy."

"You are sure?" Hamilton asked.

"He had no connection to *her*. They might have been friendly, but you can be assured—*without question*—that he did not feel betrayed by her loving either of the boys who claim to love Rachael and be loved by her."

Violet blinked and reexamined Marcus Irons, who blushed but didn't look away from the board. The things they listed under his name were all fiction as far as they knew, having next to no information about him, but he didn't even seem all that upset by them. Violet watched him carefully. They had gotten his story entirely wrong, Violet thought. If her suspicion was correct about Marcus, he had no reason to kill Miss Morgan.

Violet examined him, examined Snag, and then said, "Perhaps Mr. Allen was incorrect about Marcus. I doubt it was the same for these rest of these men. This Elijah Ballard fellow thought he could compliment the shut-in niece of his professor and escape with her heart and her money—emphasis on the money. The same with Tanner, I think. Scholarship boy with an earnest gaze, it would have appealed to a girl who barely escaped her uncle's thumb."

"She told you she didn't love you," Tanner said to Ballard. "She told you she didn't want to marry you. She *loved* me. Not him. *Me.*"

"She had cold feet," Ballard shot back. "Given time, she'd have changed her mind."

"Men," Lila muttered to Kate, who nodded. Violet glanced their way, trying to silence them, but Lila added in a louder tone, "I can assure you, sir, your Miss Morgan had a mind of her own. She'd already found you wanting. Bothering her endlessly afterwards would not have engendered caring."

"What do you know of it?" Elijah Ballard demanded, scowling at Violet and her friends.

"I'm a woman. Obviously, I know these things."

"Women's intuition?" He sneered. "Rachael didn't know what she wanted. She'd have given in eventually."

"So you were going to wear her down until she was too tired to say no again?" Lila's mocking voice made Elijah Ballard flush with anger. He glared at Lila, who only laughed. "Try it with a woman who isn't a shut-in. See if it works so well for you, idiot."

Violet shot Lila a quelling look, but she ignored it.

Thankfully for the plan, Tanner taunted Ballard again. "She didn't love you. She never was going to love you."

"Enough about the love or lack thereof of my niece," Mr. Morgan snapped. "She wasn't murdered. Her heart failed. This is all nonsense."

"My son found out otherwise," Mr. Allen the elder lied. "I paid for that research myself. The lab. Tests. The expert study."

"Anything you have is hardly reliable," Mr. Morgan shot back. "Your son wanted an outcome to support his fairy stories, and you bought it for him. That is all."

"I think..." Marcus Irons glanced at Professor Snag and then at the others. "She really was murdered?"

Hamilton looked at Marcus. "I believe she was poisoned. The slow work of the poison would have imitated her heart failing."

"You keep out of this, Mr. Irons," Mr. Morgan demanded. "This farce has gone on long enough."

Marcus swallowed, and Violet wanted to hand the lad a drink, but she didn't dare interrupt.

"If Miss Rachael was murdered," Marcus said to Daniel Morgan. "Then the information I have provides a possible motive."

"It means nothing," Mr. Morgan replied.

Marcus's face flushed, but he said, "I cannot do that, sir."

"I will see you thrown out of the program."

That silenced Marcus.

"I have an alibi for Mr. Allen's murder," Mr. Morgan continued as though he hadn't just threatened the lad. "By Jove, Hamilton. We had drinks until late."

Hamilton studied Marcus, but Morgan's threat had been too effective and the lad kept quiet, bowing his head.

"Jeremiah Allen came and found me," Mr. Tanner told them all. "He found me when I was on one of my rambles. You know about those." Tanner spoke to Professor Snag and Marcus Irons, who both nodded. "He knew about them too. He wanted something from me. We argued, but when I saw him it was after two in the morning. Perhaps you were with Mr. Morgan at that time?"

"You know we went to bed long before then, Daniel," Hamilton said.

"Did everyone know about your late night walks?" Violet asked Tanner, who glanced around those present and answered, "I think everyone but Mr. Morgan."

Violet's head cocked as she turned to Jack's friend. A picture of horror rolled out before her with an end she didn't want to know. "You know what I find most interesting all of the sudden?"

"I care not," Mr. Morgan replied.

"I care," Jack countered.

"Hamilton," Violet told Jack. "Hamilton, Jack, and Emily. If someone was killed with Hamilton Barnes of Scotland Yard in the town, of course he'd be invited to help on the case. The boys here must have been almost rabid after that clever speech of Hamilton's."

Violet turned back to Mr. Morgan, her gaze moving over him. "It was you."

"Of course it wasn't."

"You arranged the lecture," she said, not backing down as he, and his eyebrows, scowled at her.

"That means nothing more than me supporting my friend. A friendship that is over, Barnes."

"You made sure Jack was invited. You even asked us to stay with you even though Jack was going to arrange a hotel. You insisted on it. Why?"

"They're my friends. I have a large house. It means nothing."

"If that were the only piece, I'd agree with you. And yet, with the water influencing Allen's body, it would be difficult to accurately guess the time of death. Anyone would assume it would have been soon after he was removed from the reception. Did you tell him to pick a fight with Marcus? With one of your other boys? Somebody started that ruckus at Hamilton's reception. Were you behind that too?"

"You are ridiculous, my dear."

"So Hamilton and Jack are invited into the case. They already care for you. You're long-time friends. They knew Rachael personally. Knew of her heart issues. Watched you worry about her. There was no reason to link Allen's death to hers. What did he know?"

"There was nothing for him to know," Morgan told her, glancing at the others as if expecting someone to speak up for him. "Why would I kill my niece?"

"She wasn't doing want you wanted," Violet suggested, knowing that had only been part of it. She was sure—certain— she was right. It was Barnes who was the missing piece, not anything else.

"Hardly motive for murder."

"Maybe not," Violet agreed. "Except, she was going to leave her gilded cage and go into the world with a man who could hardly give her the comforts you had. She would die slowly, leaving her money to that cad, Nathan. That wasn't what your family wanted when they entrusted their daughter to you. They wanted you to protect and love her."

"I did protect and love her."

"Even from herself," Violet challenged.

"When necessary," he snarled. "I'd never have let her marry Tanner. I didn't need to kill her to stop that."

"You know," Violet told him. "I invited the former fiancé of the man I love here today to help him. I'd do almost anything for him. It isn't even difficult for me to ignore the wishes of my family—who love me—and choose him. Your niece would have done the same. She allowed your Elijah to think he had a chance with her while making her plans with Nathan. She only needed to wait until he finished with school, and then they'd have been away."

"She wouldn't have left me. You are wrong."

"What did you do to your fortune?" Violet asked. "Where did it go?"

Mr. Morgan stumbled then. It was apparent he hadn't expected her to change tactics so suddenly.

"I can find out, of course. I'm good at money."

"You're a woman."

"That is also true," Violet told him.

"He lost it," Marcus said suddenly. "He invested heavily with his cash into a scheme and it all fell apart. He was ruined. It was why he let Jeremiah's father buy the fool's way into the program. Professor Morgan sent him a list of things they needed, and Allen wrote a check. Simple. Easy. Then Rachael died, and he got most of that too. He had been on the brink of ruin."

"You can't prove any of this," Morgan snarled.

Jack stared at his friend. "My God, Daniel. Rachael adored you. How could you kill her?"

"I didn't."

"Where is your cane?" Jack demanded. "You had it the evening of the reception. I hadn't realized you'd stopped using it. We'll find it. It'll match young Jeremiah's wound, and it'll all be over. Now that we know what to look for—"

Morgan shoved his chair back and ran.

"Oh, by Jove!" Denny cheered. "Lila, did you see?"

The door to the hotel suite banged against the wall as it flew open. Denny ran after Mr. Morgan but collided with Jack. Mr. Morgan, however, was tackled by the local police officers that Hamilton had at the ready.

The rest of them crowded behind Jack and Denny and watched as the local police took Morgan away with Hamilton following after, explaining what had occurred.

"Sorry about nearly knocking you down, old man." Denny clapped Jack on the shoulder. "I was feeling a bit high-spirited."

"Why did he run?" Victor asked. "He might have bluffed his way through it if he hadn't run."

Violet and Jack glanced at each other and then back at Victor. "The cane," they said together.

"Stupid man," Jack muttered. "He might have gotten away with if it wasn't someplace we could find it."

"He was sure of us," Hamilton Barnes said. "Sure we'd never think of him. He loved that cane."

"We wouldn't have suspected him," Jack said, sounding disgusted. "If not for Jeremy. The boy must have gotten at least one thing right to prompt his murder when he was stumbling around investigating Miss Morgan's death."

"Oh," Professor Snag said, "Jeremiah Allen was right more often than you would think. Lord Pemberton's son was stealing Jeremy's money from his rooms. The religion student really did have associations with brothel girls, though running a brothel was a bit far-fetched. Professor Gregory Naveen was removed when the dean realized that he was, in fact, selling his test questions to any student with the means to pay."

Violet blinked.

"Mr. Allen paid attention, read all the journal articles, followed all the cases. He was quite brilliant. Just young and in need of molding."

"What did he suspect you of?" Violet asked Professor Snag, remembering that Jeremiah Allen had searched Professor Snag's office.

The professor grinned wickedly, his kind eyes twinkling. "I'll never tell."

CHAPTER TWENTY

The shoreline curled out into the sea with a stiff breeze over the cool water. Violet held her shoes in her hand, and her skirts were wet at the hem from walking along the shore.

"That was freezing," Violet told Jack, grinning up at the mountain of him. His broad shoulders blocked the sun and gave her shade despite the gloriously sunny day. Rouge ran along the sea, barking at the waves. Other than Violet's spaniel, they were alone.

Jack tangled their fingers together. "I wasn't sure I would remember what it felt like to be cold, but that reminded me."

His pants were rolled up to his calves, and they were as wet as the hem of Violet's dress.

"I didn't think you would make it while we were still here," Violet admitted. "I thought you'd have to carry on with the case."

Jack shrugged. "The dean shamed Daniel into confessing after laying out the evidence. Once we knew where to look, it wasn't that hard to find. Daniel had gotten his friend at the journal to invite Ham to write his article and then arranged the event. We found the cane. It matched the wound. The fool even purchased the poison himself. When Emily's first article was published, a chemist came forward. As soon as we put it all together, we had only to fill in the missing pieces."

Violet adjusted her hat, holding it on her head when a stiff wind threatened to carry it away. "I'm sorry it was your friend."

"I'm sorry he used our friendship to hide his crimes." Jack cleared his throat and then took a stone from his pocket, throwing it out to sea. "Emily asked me to forgive her. She said she'd repented her mistake and had always regretted it."

Violet knew what his answer had been and the only feeling she had about Jack's statement was sympathy for Emily Allen. The woman hadn't recognized what she'd had until it was too late. Violet would not be so foolish.

Jack turned to Violet, tilting her face to his. "You didn't doubt me when Emily came around. Even now, you knew I had turned her away."

Violet lifted her brow and waited.

"I doubted you when I saw you with Tomas and saw he loved you. I was so jealous it was like a fire in my gut. I—" Jack thrust his hands into his pockets. "I am always going to be protective of you, Violet. Jealous even. I'm always going to worry that someone will snatch you away from me. It happened with Emily. I *know* you aren't her, but I love you so much more than I ever loved her. She broke me. If it were you, Vi, I wouldn't survive."

Violet pressed her lips together, hating the agony that the mere thought of her betrayal put in his voice.

"I won't doubt you, not really," he assured her. "I know you would never actually betray me."

"I would never."

"I know," Jack said. "I'm messing this up again. I..."

Violet waited. She had been determined to hear it again. For it to be all hers this time. No dead bodies, no case, nothing but the two of them.

"You give me joy." Jack rubbed his hand over his mouth as if surprised to hear the words coming from his mouth. "And laughter. You've taught me to like stupid books like *Tarzan* and *Bulldog Drummond*."

Violet pressed her lips together to hold back a reply. She wanted the words. All of them. It was only fair.

"I didn't know I could love so hard until you." It was then that he slipped to his knees, taking her hand to press a ring into her palm. "I don't have poetry, or clever words, or grand romantic gestures. All I can give you is my heart, a solemn vow to adore you the rest of my days, and the very disturbing promise that if you say no, I'll just keep asking until you're worn out."

Violet laughed a watery laugh. She slipped to her knees in front of him, letting the water wet her dress further as small waves covered their legs. She put the ring on her finger without looking away from his face. It was his expression and his words that she wanted. The love in his gaze.

"You've already worn me down." She cupped his jaw in her hand, looking into his eyes and seeing her own face reflected back. "I'm already yours. Didn't you know?"

"I want the words, Violet. I know what they mean to you. I know what giving them to me will mean to you."

She waited, giving him a merry but tear-filled smile.

He knew what she wanted, and he gave it to her. "Will you marry me, Lady Violet Carlyle? Will you be mine?"

She let her thumb run over his bottom lip, reveling in this moment. "Yes. Of course I will."

Jack kissed her then, fiercely, stealing her breath. He already had her heart, but he took her breath too.

Violet wasn't sure how much time passed when Denny called, "Finally."

She gasped, pressing her face into Jack's chest only to tilt her head to the side and peek out to see if Denny was really there. It wasn't *just* that fool. It was her twin, Kate, Denny, *and* Lila. Violet gaped at their grinning faces and then glanced at Jack, who was as surprised as she.

"We have been waiting and waiting," Denny said cheerily over the sound of the wind, waves, and birds. "I mean, you couldn't have taken a few minutes in Oxford to wrap it up? We had to come all the way to Dorset to secure this deal?"

"Shut up, my lad," Lila said, elbowing her husband. "You know Violet can be vicious."

"I told you he was going to propose," Denny said, ignoring his wife. "I thought he had us beat with the boat thing. The whole taking Vi off to Oxford was damned clever. Kept us from witnessing his begging, unlike Victor."

"It didn't look like begging to me," Kate said with a wide smile. "It looked just lovely. We're sorry. We're terrible friends."

"They knew that already," Victor told Kate. He was grinning so widely, Violet thought his face just might crack. "Jack's supposed to be a bright lad. He should have realized we'd follow them down. We all knew it was coming. Even Violet did. Look at her dress. Sets off her hair, makes her cheeks all rosy. Look at her wearing that pink lipstick. It's Jack's favorite."

"Jack's wearing it now," Denny inserted, and Kate bit back a laugh.

"Careful, my love," Lila told her husband. "Jack might decide to teach you a lesson."

"We lads have to stick together and give a head's up when we're wearing our girl's lipstick. It's a man thing, love. You wouldn't understand."

"What is so hard to understand about that?" Lila demanded, rolling her eyes at him. "Sometimes I wonder why I love you."

"Wore you down, don't you remember?" Denny asked her. "Just like Jack threatened. That was my favorite bit." An excited expression crossed Denny's face as though he'd discovered a great treasure. "This calls for champagne. Or cocktails. Or champagne cocktails. Definitely chocolates though. Let's go get some while Jack cleans up his face."

Denny went ahead of the others towards where they were staying, and the rest gave the couple one last look before they followed, with Victor even whistling for Vi's dog.

"Do we have to keep them?" Jack asked, pushing to his feet and pulling Violet up with him. His arm was firm around her waist, and her feet dangled over the water.

Violet wrapped her arms around his shoulders. "If we leave them," she asked Jack seriously, "who would care for them?"

"So it's for the good of mankind?" He smiled at her as though there were something precious in her that only he could see.

"I'm afraid so."

He looked back over his shoulder and saw they'd truly left, then he tilted her chin up to him with his free hand. "Perhaps you can make it up to me?"

Violet endeavored to do her best.

THE END

Hullo, my friends, I have so much gratitude for you reading my books. Almost as wonderful as giving me a chance are reviews, and indie folks, like myself, need them desperately! If you wouldn't mind, I would be so grateful for a review.

The sequel to this book, Gin & Murder, is available now.

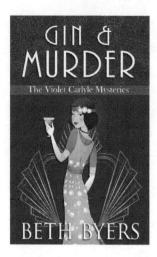

September 1924.

When Violet and Victor are called home to account for their actions, only one course of action is possible. They pack a liberal amount of alcohol and call on their friends to rally round.

They've been outed as writers of sensational fiction! Of falling in love with unapproved individuals! They've bought houses while drunk and had the gall to get sucked into murder investigations! And, it was Violet who was credited with helping to find the killers! The explosion is a story for the ages.

To say that no one expected a body soaked in gin is a stretch after what these friends have been through. The real shocker is when the earl asks Jack, Violet, Victor, and their friends to solve the murder and save what remains of the family's good name.

Order Here.

If you enjoy mysteries with a historical twist, scroll to the end for a sample of my new mystery series, The Poison Ink Mysteries. The first book, Death by The Book, is available now.

Inspired by classic fiction and Miss Buncle's Book. Death by the Book questions what happens when you throw a murder into idyllic small town England.

July 1936

When Georgette Dorothy Marsh's dividends fall along with the banks, she decides to write a book. Her only hope is to bring her account out of overdraft and possibly buy some hens. The problem is that she has so little imagination she uses her neighbors for inspiration.

She little expects anyone to realize what she's done. So when *Chronicles of Harper's Bend* becomes a bestseller, her neighbors are questing to find out just who this "Joseph Johns" is and punish him.

Things escalate beyond what anyone would imagine when one of her prominent characters turns up dead. It seems that the fictional end Georgette had written for the character spurred a real-life murder. Now to find the killer before it is discovered who the author is and she becomes the next victim.

Order Here.

If you want book updates, you could follow me on Facebook where you'll find cover reveals, sneak peeks, and news.

ALSO BY BETH BYERS

The Violet Carlyle Cozy Historical Mysteries

Murder & the Heir

Murder at Kennington House

Murder at the Folly

A Merry Little Murder

New Year's Madness: A Short Story Anthology

Valentine's Madness: A Short Story Anthology

Murder Among the Roses

Murder in the Shallows

Gin & Murder

Obsidian Murder

Murder at the Ladies Club

Weddings Vows & Murder

A Jazzy Little Murder

Murder by Chocolate

A Friendly Little Murder

Murder by the Sea

Murder On All Hallows

The Poison Ink Mysteries

Death By the Book

Death Witnessed

Death by Blackmail (available for preorder)

Death Misconstrued (available for preorder)

Deathly Ever After

The 2nd Chance Diner Mysteries

(This is a completed series.)

Spaghetti, Meatballs, & Murder

Cookies & Catastrophe

Poison & Pie

Double Mocha Murder

Cinnamon Rolls & Cyanide

Tea & Temptation

Donuts & Danger

Scones & Scandal

Lemonade & Loathing

Wedding Cake & Woe

Honeymoons & Honeydew

The Pumpkin Problem

DEATH BY THE BOOK PREVIEW

Chapter One

GEORGETTE MARSH

*G*eorgette Dorothy Marsh stared at the statement from her bank with a dawning horror. The dividends had been falling, but this...this wasn't livable. She bit down on the inside of her lip and swallowed frantically. *What was she going to do?* Tears were burning in the back of her eyes, and her heart was racing frantically.

There wasn't enough for—for—anything. Not for cream for her tea or resoling her shoes or firewood for the winter. Georgette glanced out the window, remembered it was spring, and realized that something must be done.

Something, but *what*?

"Miss?" Eunice said from the doorway, "the tea at Mrs. Wilkes is this afternoon. You asked me to remind you."

Georgette nodded, frantically trying to hide her tears from

her maid, but the servant had known Georgette since the day of her birth, caring for her from her infancy to the current day.

"What has happened?"

"The...the dividends," Georgette breathed. She didn't have enough air to speak clearly. "The dividends. It's not enough."

Eunice's head cocked as she examined her mistress and then she said, "Something must be done."

"But what?" Georgette asked, biting down on her lip again. *Hard.*

CHARLES AARON

"Uncle?"

Charles Aaron glanced up from the stack of papers on his desk at his nephew some weeks after Georgette Marsh had written her book in a fury of desperation. It was Robert Aaron who had discovered the book, and it was Charles Aaron who would give it life.

Robert had been working at Aaron & Luther Publishing House for a year before Georgette's book appeared in the mail, and he read the slush pile of books that were submitted by new authors before either of the partners stepped in. It was an excellent rewarding work when you found that one book that separated itself from the pile, and Robert got that thrill of excitement every time he found a book that had a touch of *something*. It was the very feeling that had Charles himself pursuing a career in publishing and eventually creating his own firm.

It didn't seem to matter that Charles had his long history of discovering authors and their books. Familiarity had most definitely *not* led to contempt. He was, he had to admit, in love with reading—fiction especially—and the creative mind. He had learned that some of the books he found would speak only to him.

Often, however, some he loved would become best sellers. With the best sellers, Charles felt he was sharing a delightful secret with the world. There was magic in discovering a new writer. A contagious sort of magic that had infected Robert. There was nothing that Charles enjoyed more than hearing someone recommend a book he'd published to another.

"You've found something?"

Robert shrugged, but he also handed the manuscript over a smile right on the edge of his lips and shining eyes that flicked to the manuscript over and over again. "Yes, I think so." He wasn't confident enough yet to feel certain, but Charles had noticed for some time that Robert was getting closer and closer to no longer needing anyone to guide him.

"I'll look it over soon."

It was the end of the day and Charles had a headache building behind his eyes. He always did on the days when he had to deal with the bestseller Thomas Spencer. He was too successful for his own good and expected any publishing company to bend entirely to his will.

Robert watched Charles load the manuscript into his satchel, bouncing just a little before he pulled back and cleared his throat. The boy—man, Charles supposed—smoothed his suit, flashed a grin, and left the office. Leaving for the day wasn't a bad plan. He took his satchel and—as usual—had dinner at his club before retiring to a corner of the room with an overstuffed armchair, an Old-Fashioned, and his pipe.

Charles glanced around the club, noting the other regulars. Most of them were bachelors who found it easier to eat at the club than to employ a cook. Every once in a while there was a family man who'd escaped the house for an evening with the gents, but for the most part—it was bachelors like himself.

When Charles opened the neat pages of 'Joseph Jones's *The Chronicles of Harper's Bend,* he intended to read only a small portion of the book. To get a feel for what Robert had seen and perhaps determine whether it was worth a more thorough look. After a few pages, Charles decided upon just a few more. A few more pages after that, and he left his club to return home and finish the book by his own fire.

It might have been early summer, but they were also in the middle of a ferocious storm. Charles preferred the crackle of fire wherever possible when he read, as well as a good cup of tea. There was no question that the book was well done. There was no question that Charles would be contacting the author and making an offer on the book. *The Chronicles of Harper's Bend* was, in fact, so captivating in its honesty, he couldn't quite decide whether this author loved the small towns of England or despised them. He rather felt it might be both.

Either way, it was quietly sarcastic and so true to the little village that raised Charles Aaron that he felt he might turn the page and discover the old woman who'd lived next door to his parents or the vicar of the church he'd attended as a boy. Charles felt as though he knew the people stepping off the pages.

Yes, Charles thought, yes. This one, he thought, *this* would be a best seller. Charles could feel it in his bones. He tapped out his pipe into the ashtray. This would be one of those books he looked back on with pride at having been the first to know that this book was the next big thing. Despite the lateness of the hour, Charles approached his bedroom with an energized delight. A letter would be going out in the morning.

GEORGETTE MARSH

It was on the very night that Charles read the *Chronicles* that Miss Georgette Dorothy Marsh paced, once again, in front of her fireplace. The wind whipped through the town of Bard's Crook sending a flurry of leaves swirling around the graves in the small churchyard and then shooing them down to a small lane off of High Street where the elderly Mrs. Henry Parker had been awake for some time. She had woken worried over her granddaughter who was recovering too slowly from the measles.

The wind rushed through the cottages at the end of the lane, causing the gate at the Wilkes house to rattle. Dr. Wilkes and his wife were curled up together in their bed sharing warmth in the face of the changing weather. A couple much in love, snuggling into their beds on a windy evening was a joy for them both.

The leaves settled into a pile in the corner of the picket fence right at the very last cottage on that lane of Miss Georgette Dorothy Marsh. Throughout most of Bard's Crook, people were sleeping. Their hot water bottles were at the ends of their beds, their blankets were piled high, and they went to bed prepared for another day. The unseasonable chill had more than one household enjoying a warm cup of milk at bedtime, though not Miss Marsh's economizing household.

Miss Marsh, unlike the others, was not asleep. She didn't have a fire as she was quite at the end of her income and every adjustment must be made. If she were going to be honest with herself, and she very much didn't want to be—she was past the end of her income. Her account had become overdraft, her dividends had dried up, and it might be time to recognize that her last-ditch effort of writing a book about her neighbors had not been successful.

She had looked at the lives of folks like Anthony Trollope who both worked and wrote novels and Louisa May Alcott who wrote to relieve the stress of her life and to help bring in financial help. As much as Georgette loved to read, and she did, she loved the idea that somewhere out there an author was using their art to restart their lives. There was a romance to being a writer, but she wondered just how many writers were pragmatic behind the fairy-tales they crafted. It wasn't, Georgette thought, going to be her story like Louisa May Alcott. Georgette was going to do something else.

"Miss Georgie," Eunice said, "I can hear you. You'll catch something dreadful if you don't sleep." The sound of muttering chased Georgie, who had little doubt Eunice was complaining about catching something dreadful herself.

"I'm sorry, Eunice," Georgie called. "I—" Georgie opened the door to her bedroom and faced the woman. She had worked for Mr. and Mrs. Marsh when Georgie had been born and in all the years of loss and change, Eunice had never left Georgie. Even now when the economies made them both uncomfortable. "Perhaps—"

"It'll be all right in the end, Miss Georgie. Now to bed with you."

Georgette did not, however, go to bed. Instead, she pulled out her pen and paper and listed all of the things she might do to further economize. They had a kitchen garden already, and it provided the vast majority of what they ate. They did their own mending and did not buy new clothes. They had one goat that they milked and made their own cheese. Though Georgette had to recognize that she rather feared goats. They were, of all creatures, devils. They would just randomly knock one over.

Georgie shivered and refused to consider further goats. Perhaps she could tutor someone? She thought about those she knew and realized that no one in Bard's Crook would hire the quiet Georgette Dorothy Marsh to influence their children. The village's wallflower and cipher? Hardly a legitimate option for any caring parent. Georgette was all too aware of what her neighbors thought of her. She rose again, pacing more quietly as she considered and rejected her options.

Georgie paced until quite late and then sat down with her pen and paper and wondered if she should try again with her writing. Something else. Something with more imagination. She had started her book with fits until she'd landed on practicing writing by describing an episode of her village. It had grown into something more, something beyond Bard's Crook with just conclusions to the lives she saw around her.

When she'd started *The Chronicles of Harper's Bend,* she had been more desperate than desirous of a career in writing. Once again, she recognized that she must do something and she wasn't well-suited to anything but writing. There were no typist jobs in Bard's Crook, no secretarial work. The time when rich men paid for companions for their wives or elderly mothers was over, and the whole of the world was struggling to survive, Georgette included.

She'd thought of going to London for work, but if she left her snug little cottage, she'd have to pay for lodging elsewhere. Georgie sighed into her palm and then went to bed. There was little else to do at that moment. Something, however, must be done.

DEATH BY THE BOOK PREVIEW

Chapter Two

*T*hree days later, the day dawned with a return to summer, and the hills were rolling out from Bard's Crook as though being whispered over by the gods themselves. It seemed all too possible that Aurora had descended from Olympus to smile on the village. Miss Marsh's solitary hen with her cold, hard eyes was click-clacking around the garden, eating her seeds, and generally disgusting the lady of the house.

Miss Marsh had woken to the sound of newspaper boy arriving, but she had dressed rather leisurely. There was little to look forward to outside of a good cup of tea, light on the sugar, and without cream. She told herself she preferred her tea without cream, but in the quiet of her bedroom, she could admit that she very much wanted cream in her tea. If Georgie could persuade a god to her door, it would be the goddess Fortuna to bless Georgie's book and provide enough ready money to afford cream and better teas. Was her life even worth living with the watered-down muck she'd been forced to drink lately?

Georgette put on her dress, which had been old when it had

been given to her and was the perfect personification of dowdiness. She might also add to her dream list, enough money for a dress or two. By Jove, she thought, how wonderful would a hat be? A lovely new one? Or perhaps a coat that fit her? The list of things that needed to be replaced in her life was near endless.

She sighed into the mirror glancing over her familiar face with little emotion. She neither liked nor disliked her face. She knew her hair was pretty enough though it tended towards a frizziness she'd never learned to anticipate or tame. The color was a decent medium brown with corresponding medium brown eyes. Her skin was clear of blemishes, for which she was grateful, though she despised the freckles that sprinkled over her nose and cheeks. Her dress rose to her collar, but her freckles continued down her arms and over her chest. At least her lips were perfectly adequate, neither thin nor full, but nothing to cause a second glance. Like all of her, she thought, there was nothing to cause a second glance.

Despite her lackluster looks, she didn't despise her face. She rather liked herself. Unlike many she knew, the inside of her head was not a terrible place to be. She had no major regrets and enjoyed her own humor well enough even if she rarely bothered to share her thoughts with others.

Georgette supposed if she had been blessed with liveliness, she might be rather pretty, but she knew herself well. She was quiet. Both in her persona and voice, and she was easily ignored. It had never been something that she bemoaned. She was who she was and though very few knew her well, those who knew her liked her. Those who knew her well—the very few who could claim such a status—liked her very well.

On a morning when Georgie was not worrying over her bank account, she could be counted on entering the dining room at 9:00 a.m. On that morning, however, she was rather late. She had

considered goats again as she brushed her teeth—no one else in
Bard's Crook kept goats though there were several who kept
cows. Those bedamned goats kept coming back to her mind, but
she'd rather sell everything she owned and throw herself on the
mercy of the city than keep goats. She had considered trying to
sew clothing while she'd pulled on her stockings and slipped her
shoes on her feet. She had considered whether she might make
hats when she'd brushed her hair, and she had wondered if she
might take a lodger as she'd straightened her dress and exited her
bedroom.

All of her options were rejected before she reached the base
of her stairs, and she entered the dining room with an edge of
desperation. As she took her seat at the head of the table and
added a very small amount of sugar to her weak tea, her attention
was caught by the most unexpected of sights. A letter to the left
of her plate. Georgette lifted it with shaking hands and read the
return address. Aaron & Luther Publishing. She gasped and then
slowly blew out the air.

"Be brave, dear girl," she whispered, as she cut open the enve-
lope. "If they say no, you can always send your book to Anderson
Books. Hope is not gone. Not yet."

She pulled the single sheet of paper out and wondered if it
was a good sign or a bad sign that they had not returned her
book. Slowly, carefully, she unfolded the letter, her tea and toast
entirely abandoned as she read the contents.

Moments later, the letter fluttered down to her plate and she
sipped her scalding hot tea and didn't notice the burn.

"Is all well, Miss Georgie?" The maid was standing in the
doorway. Her wrinkled face was fixated on her girl with the same
tense anticipation that had Georgette reading her letter over and
over while it lay open on her plate. Those dark eyes were fixated
on Georgette's face with careful concern.

"I need cream, Eunice." Georgette nodded to her maid. "We're saved. They want *Chronicles*. My goodness, my *dear, wonderful* woman, see to the cream and let's stop making such weak tea until we discover the details of the fiscal benefits."

Eunice had to have been as relieved as Georgette, but the maid simply nodded stalwartly and came back into the dining room a few minutes later with a fresh pot of strong tea, a full bowl of sugar, and the cream that had been intended for supper. It was still the cheapest tea that was sold in Bard's Crook, but it was black and strong and tasted rather like nirvana on her tongue when Georgette drank it down.

"I'll go up to London tomorrow. He wants to see me in the afternoon, but he states very clearly he wants the book. We're saved."

"Don't count your chickens before they hatch, Miss Georgie."

"By Jove, we aren't just saved from a lack of cream, Eunice. We're saved from goats! We're saved my dear. Have a seat and enjoy a cuppa yourself."

Eunice clucked and returned to the kitchen instead. They might be saved, but the drawing room still needed to be done, dinner still needed to be started, and the laundry and mending were waiting for no woman.

When Miss Marsh made her way into London the following day, she was wearing her old cloche, which was quite dingy but the best she had, a coat that was worn at the cuffs and the hem, and shoes that were just starting to have a hole worn into the bottom. Perhaps, she thought, there would even be enough to re-sole her shoes.

On the train into London from Bard's Crook, only Mr.

Thornton was taking the train from the village. When he inquired after her business, she quite shocked herself when she made up a story about meeting an old Scottish school chum for tea. Mr. Thornton admitted he intended to meet with his lawyer. He was rather notorious in Bard's Crook for changing his will as often as the wind changed direction. An event he always announced with an air of doom and a frantic waggling of his eyebrows.

Mr. Thornton had married a woman from the factories who refused to acknowledge her past, and together they had three children. Those children—now adults—included two rebellious sons and one clinging daughter. He also had quite a slew of right-eous nephews who deserved the acclaim they received. Whenever his wife bullied him too hard or his sons rebelled too overtly, the will altered in favor of the righteous nephews until such time as an appropriate repentance could be made.

Georgie had long since taken to watching the flip-flopping of the will with a delighted air. As far as she could tell, no one but herself enjoyed the changing of his will, but enjoying things that others didn't seem to notice had long been her fate.

The fortunate news of the inheritance situation was that Mr. Thornton's nephews were unaware of the changing of their fortunes. The clinging daughter's fortune was set in stone. She never rebelled and thus never had her fortunes reversed, but she clung rather too fiercely to be a favored inheritor.

Mr. Thornton handed Miss Marsh down from the train, offered to share a black cab, and then left her without regret when she made a weak excuse. Miss Marsh selected her own black cab, cutting into her ready money dreadfully, and hoped that whatever occurred today would restore her cash in hand.

CHARLES AARON

"Mr. Aaron," Schmidt said, "your afternoon appointment has arrived."

"Wonderful," Charles replied. "Send him in with tea, will you Schmidtty?"

"Her, sir."

"Her? Isn't my appointment with an author?" Charles felt a flash of irritation. He was very much looking forward to meeting the author of *The Chronicles of Harper's Bend*. He had, in fact, read the book twice more since that first time.

Schmidt's lips twitched when he said, "It seems the author is a Miss Marsh."

Charles thought over the book and realized that of course Mr. Jones was a Miss Marsh. Who but a woman would realize the fierce shame of bribing one's children with candies to behave for church? Charles could almost hear the tirade of his grandmother about the lack of mothering skills in the upcoming generations.

"Well, send her in, and tea as well." Charles rubbed his hands together in glee. He did adore meeting new writers. They were never what you expected, but they all had one thing in common. Behind their dull or beautiful faces, behind their polite smiles and small talk, there were whole worlds. Characters with secrets that only the writer knew. Unnecessary histories that were cut viciously from the story and hidden away only to be known by the author.

Charles rather enjoyed asking the writers random questions about their characters' secret histories. Tell me, author, Charles would say, as they shared a cup of tea or a pipe, what does so-and-so do on Christmas morning? Or what is his/her favorite color? He loved when they answered readily, knowing that of course so-and-so woke early on Christmas morning, opened presents and had a rather spectacular full English only to sleep it off on the Chesterfield near the fire.

He loved it when they described what they ate down to the nearest detail as though the character's traditional breakfast had been made since time immemorial rather than born with a pen and hidden behind the gaze of the person with whom Charles was sharing an hour or two.

Charles had long since become inured to the varying attitudes of authors. Thomas Spencer, who had given Charles a rather terrible headache that had been cured by Miss Marsh's delightful book, wore dandified clothes and had an arrogant air. Spencer felt the cleverness of his books justified his rudeness.

On the other hand, an even more brilliant writer, Henry Moore, was a little man with a large stomach. He kept a half-dozen cats, spoiled his children terribly, and was utterly devoted to his wife. In a gathering of authors, Moore would be the most successful and the cleverest by far but be overshadowed by every other writer in attendance.

Miss Marsh, Charles saw, fell into the 'Moore' category. She seemed as timid as a newborn rabbit as she edged into his office. Her gaze flit about, taking in the stack of manuscripts, the shelf of books he'd published over the course of his career, the windows that looked onto a dingy alleyway, and the large wooden desk.

She was, he thought, a dowdy little thing. Her eyes were nice enough, but they barely met his own, and she didn't seem to know quite what to say. Her freckles seemed to be rather spectac-ular—if one liked freckles—but it was hard to anything with her timid movements. Especially with her face barely meeting his own. That was all right, he thought, he'd done this many times, and she was very new to the selling of a book and the signing of contracts.

"Hello," he said rather cheerily, hoping that his tone would set her at ease.

She glanced up at him and then back down, her gaze darting around his office again. Mr. Aaron wondered just what she was seeing amidst all of his things. He wouldn't be surprised to find she was noting things that the average fellow would overlook.

"Would you like tea?"

Miss Marsh nodded, and he poured her a cup to which she added a hefty amount of cream and sugar. He grinned at the sight of her milky tea and then leaned back as she slowly spun her teacup on the saucer.

"Why Joseph Jones? Why a pen name at all?"

Miss Marsh blinked rather rapidly and then admitted, "Well..." Her gaze darted to the side, and she said, "I was rather inspired by my neighbors, but I would prefer to avoid their gossip as well. Can you imagine?" A cheeky grin crossed her face for a moment, and he was entranced. "If they discovered that Antoinette Moore wrote a book?"

"Is that you?"

"Pieces of her," she admitted, and he frowned. The quiet woman in front of him certainly had the mannerisms of the character, but he couldn't quite see Miss Moore writing a book and sending it off. She was such an innocuous, almost unnecessary character in the book.

Was Miss Marsh was a literary portraitist? He grinned at the idea and wanted nothing more than to visit Harper's Bend or wherever it was that this realistic portrayal existed in real life. What he would give to have an afternoon tea with the likes of Mrs. Morton and her ilk.

Mr. Aaron glanced over Miss Marsh. Her old cloche and worn coat were not lost on him, and he supposed if he'd met her anywhere else he'd never have looked at her twice. Having read her book, however, he suddenly felt as though she were far more charming than she'd otherwise have been.

Her gaze, with ordinary medium brown eyes, seemed to have untold depths, and her freckles seemed to be an outward indicator of a woman who could look at her village and turn it into a witty caricature, acting as a warning that this was a woman who said nothing and noticed everything.

He grinned at her. "I read your book, and I liked it."

Her eyes flashed and a bright grin crossed her face, and he realized she was a little prettier than he'd noticed. It was that shocked delight on her face that made him add, "I like it quite well indeed."

Miss Marsh clasped her hands tightly together, and Mr. Aaron did not miss how her grip camouflaged the trembling of her hands.

"Tell me about it," he said kindly. "Why did you write it? This is a portrait of your neighbors?"

It was the kindness that got Miss Marsh to open up, and then she couldn't seem to stem the tide of her thoughts; they sped out. "Well, it was my dividends you see. They've quite dried up. I was struggling before, but they'd always come in and then they didn't, and I was quite—" Miss Marsh trailed off and Mr. Aaron could imagine the situation all too easily. "at my wit's end. Only then I thought of Louisa May Alcott and the other lady writers, and I thought I might as well try as not."

The world was struggling and Miss Marsh, who may have escaped the early failing of things, had eventually succumbed as so many had. As she said, her dividends had dried up. He could imagine her lying awake worried and uncertain or perhaps pacing her home. There was something so unpretentious about her revelation that Mr. Aaron was even more charmed. She'd come to the end of things, and she'd turned that worry into the most charming of stories. Not just a charming story, but one filled with heart and delight in the little things. He liked her all the better for it.

If you enjoyed this sample, the book is available for purchase on Amazon or for free through Kindle Unlimited.

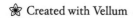

Made in the USA
San Bernardino, CA
16 September 2019